CW01665800

HOOKED

SARAH CONWAY

authors
AND CO.

ISBN13 Paperback: 978-1-913728-93-9

ISBN13 Hardback: 978-1-913728-94-6

CHAPTER ONE

In my defence, Jed seemed okay in the dark.

I'd taken a few years out, ticking off stuff from my bucket list, then decided it was time to embark on a degree. Because of my time at the 'University of Life' I was often the oldest person in the lesson. This house party was no different.

I was feeling the age gap that evening. I was twenty-three – five years older than some of the students there. Jed was one of the few people that I spied from my vantage point on the stairs that seemed a similar age. He must have sensed me watching because he came over and sat next to me.

"Alright?" he asked by way of introduction.

"Alright?" I replied. I had a knack for new languages.

The thick smell of cigarettes that hung in the air disguised Jed's own distinct odour. I'd also had a few Red Stripes and a bottle of 20/20 so I found him quite funny. At the end of the night, we had a deceptively promising snog and he asked for my number.

That meeting led to a relationship that lasted way beyond his use-by date. Whenever I'm asked if there's anything I regret or would change, he's always top of the list.

It's not that I didn't see the red flags or hear the alarm bells that waved and clanged the entire time we were together. I simply had some warped notion that it was better to ignore them than suffer the constant disappointment of being left, yet again, to walk home alone. When he started talking to me at the party, I was flattered by the attention. Finally, I'd been chosen.

Our first date was at a Wetherspoons on 'Pound-a-Pint Student Night'.

"Y'alright?" he said.

"Yep." I needed a beer. I was sure we'd get on great after a beer.

Five beers later, my prediction came true. He was studying photography, having dropped out of Sport Science after one term.

"Too much science, not enough sport," he said.

He didn't ask, but I told him I was studying Law.

"Cool," he said. "Ally McBeal was *hot*!"

I took a swig of beer. Was that a compliment?

"You know, I normally fancy blondes but you're actually pretty fit."

I'm a brunette with just-past-the-shoulder hair and, so I've been told, lovely brown eyes.

"And I normally go for bigger tits."

I'm a well-proportioned size ten – my boobs were never going to be massive. For the record, I also liked my lips, legs and ears (who doesn't like their ears) and I have a wicked sense of humour.

I looked at Jed. Tall, slim (borderline skinny) with a well-balanced face and blond hair that had been styled to make it look like it hadn't been styled. Incidentally, I was also taking a walk on the wild side as I usually went for dark hair and a bigger build. I say 'usually'... in truth, my love life had always been more *intermittent* than *usual.*

I ignored Jed's distinct personality because sadly, the idea of having someone at the end of the night was definitely more appealing than Jed himself. Nevertheless, we slept together after about two weeks, which is about six months in student time. Then followed a six-week sub-optimal association (*relationship* would have been pushing it) that was easier than dumping him or returning to the way things used to be.

Up until our last evening together, the sex had been harmless enough. I never came but didn't expect to. He would make a fumbled attempt at foreplay, and I would groan a bit rather than educate him. After that we would partake in ten minutes of missionary, and then he would come, roll over and fall straight to sleep. I would have a shower, come back to bed and fall asleep in the little bit of space that Jed had left me. At some point in the night, he would sneak out; a fact that I was secretly grateful for as I couldn't imagine having to make conversation over breakfast like we were a proper boyfriend and girlfriend.

On what turned out to be our last evening, Jed texted me at about 8 pm, which was strange as we normally just met up in town towards the end of the evening.

> 'U in' – he asked.
> 'Yes. You okay?'
> 'C U in 20.'

I ran upstairs to have a quick shower and shave where necessary.

When Jed arrived he was acting weird and was all over me from the moment he came in.

"Are you high?" I asked.

He ignored me.

"You smell great," he said, as he nuzzled and groped.

He manoeuvred me towards the stairs, hands everywhere and planting sloppy kisses on my neck. It wasn't refined but I'd not seen his attentive side before and I was intrigued as to where it would lead. Entwined, we climbed the stairs and he closed my bedroom door with a kick. Then, carried away by the enthusiasm I was seemingly responsible for, I unbuckled Jed's trousers and reached inside.

"Take off your top," Jed said. "Let me see your tits."

I dutifully removed my t-shirt and I stood proud, allowing my boobs the attention requested.

"I thought we might… you know… before we go out tonight."

Maybe today would be the day that Jed finally found my elusive clitoris. I might even help him get there.

"I've been feeling horny all day and I didn't fancy a wank."

Oh. Was I flattered that I'd just triumphed over a wank? Before I could decide, Jed placed his hands on my shoulders and applied downward pressure. Was this a massage? He pushed harder and my knees buckled. This was no massage.

"Give us a blow-job," he said. With one hand he unleashed his cock from his boxer shorts and encouraged me to kneel with the other.

1. I am not a blow-job fan and deep-throating a penis is not one of my many talents. (I was not sure I had any bedroom-based talents.)
2. I had a feeling that, unlike me, Jed had not showered in anticipation of our impromptu rendezvous.

Jed moved closer to assist me in his request.

Definitely not showered. I jumped up and performed a nifty side-step.

"I'm not in the mood," I said. There would be no clitoris-finding today.

"Fuck off," he said. "You were well up for it."

"Charlotte will be home soon." Jed wasn't to know that my roommate had actually gone home for her dad's birthday.

"Not stopped us before."

I blushed. It hadn't.

"Oh, for fuck's sake," he said as his mighty boner withered. "You're a fucking tease."

He put himself away and did up his trousers. I retrieved my t-shirt. Pride was now replaced by shame and vulnerability. I rushed to cover up.

"You know what? This is shit. I'm off to find that girl from the gym. I hear she'll suck anyone."

I do hope so, for your sake.

With that announcement, Jed left my room, my house, and my life.

Fucking twat. I looked at the clock on my bedside table: 21:12. I grabbed my bag and headed out to find somewhere where the music was loud and the drinks were Buy One Get One Free.

As luck would have it, the taxi driver knew exactly where to take me.

"You're in luck," he said. "My mate's just opened a club in town and it's Happy Hour all night."

I ignored the impossibility of that statement and ten minutes later he pulled into a taxi rank opposite a queue of what looked to be non-students. Not a Doc Marten or Fred Perry t-shirt in sight. Ordinarily, I wouldn't choose to mix with the indigenous population, but this was an emergency.

"Thanks," I paid and took a business card for later.

I took my place at the end of the queue outside *The Phoenix*, which according to the sign was 'town's newest Late Bar and Music Venue'. Once inside I made straight for the bar and ordered a tequila shot and a double vodka Red Bull. The tequila barely touched the sides but hit my knees with satisfying speed. I stuck my finger in the air.

"Same again," I said when the barman glanced over, drawing a circle in the air around the glasses in front of me.

"Rough day?" A voice to my right.

I turned and was met with denim blue eyes and eyelashes the length that men are frequently blessed with but have no need for.

"Boyfriend," I said.

"Oh," he said with a nod. "His loss."

Smooth.

"You don't even know him." Don't use throwaway compliments with me, young man.

"Don't need to." He looked me up and down and smiled.

What is it they say about finding something once you stop looking for it?

"I've just been dumped too."

I smiled and nodded. *Go on then, I'll play along.* I looked him up and down. "Her loss."

It really was her loss. My ocular travels had observed much that was worth keeping. He smelt good too. Like he actually washed and owned deodorant.

"My boyfriend was a wanker though," I said. "What about your ex?"

"Grumpy, vain." He counted on his fingers as he ran through a list of negative attributes.

"Sounds lovely," I said.

"Great tits though," he replied.

The club had started to fill up and service to slow down. We'd been waiting to be served for so long that I was beginning to think we'd moved into a blind spot.

"So, you on the rebound now then?" he asked.

Was I? Why not?

"Totally."

"Fancy a shag then? We ain't getting served any time soon."

Since when was a shag with a stranger a legitimate alternative to a tardy barman? If this was a thing, there was a pub at home where things were about to get very messy!

"Well?" It seemed he was actually expecting a considered answer.

I didn't fancy being called frigid twice in one evening and the Dutch courage had just kicked in. I replied flippantly, "Go on then. Fifty quid and I'm yours."

I was expecting him to laugh and go off in search of a freebie. No harm done, no lasting insults.

But instead, he raised his eyebrows, smirked and held out his hand. This was not the first time my big sarcastic mouth had got me into trouble.

Maybe I should have withdrawn my offer right then and put two fingers up to any potential backlash, but I thought back to earlier that evening, then to the six weeks I'd wasted with Stinky Jed, then the times I'd spent willing someone to pick me at the end of the night, then the years I'd spent playing gooseberry to my prettier friends.

At school, I wasn't the prettiest or the most popular, nor was I the sluttiest, which often trumped both the first two qualities. I was good at sport but nobody seemed to want a girlfriend based on their 800m time. After many snogs (mostly at Christmas discos) and a smattering of boyfriends that fizzled out in the time it took me to get on the Pill, I'd finally offloaded my precious virginity to a Young Farmer whilst my mum and dad were away for the weekend. I can't say I'd imagined it would take place on the lounge floor but hey, such is life.

Fuck it!

I took Blue Eyes' hand and he led me romantically to the disabled toilet.

Once inside I held out my hand for the cash (I'd watched *Pretty Woman*). Then, as I didn't want to get caught in the disabled loo (prostitution has its place but I cannot condone the abuse of facilities), I turned to the wall, pulled my knickers down, my skirt up and uttered those immortal words, "Come on then, Big Boy," to which he responded with a decent-sized cock and a not-unpleasant five minutes of penetration.

He left while I was re-doing my lippy. All I could think was, "Blimey, that's £600 an hour!"

When I woke the next morning, I was surprised for a moment to find more cash in my purse than I'd gone out with, and then I remembered how it got there. I waited to feel the morning-after shame and regret that usually followed a memory from the night before, but I felt okay. I didn't feel used, hadn't offended anyone, it hadn't been unpleasant, and I now had half of this week's rent, which was more than could be said for most of my fellow students. My mate Barney worked in a bar and would have spent all night earning the same amount.

I wondered if I'd undersold myself. What was the going rate for fourth base?

CHAPTER TWO

When I started to consider universities, I had anticipated somewhere in Scotland or Bournemouth, or maybe Leeds. Somewhere far enough away from home that I'd feel like I'd actually moved out, that the next stage of my life had started. As it happened, my first choice of course was in Cambridge, ten miles from mum and dad. I tried to deny it for a couple of weeks, desperately comparing cost, campus, and content but the answer was always the same.

To compensate, I told myself that I could pretend I lived further away and only come back at the end of each term. That plan lasted until dad dropped me off at the start of Year One and on hearing that I wouldn't be back until Christmas, insisted that I was close enough to come home more frequently.

As it turned out, it was good to be able to pop home, especially when I wanted to escape the chaos of Halls or sit in a room that smelled of Pledge rather than Pot Noodle. On the flip side, dad invited me to every social, and I felt obliged to attend.

One evening's gathering was 'cheese and wine', a loose title that masked the copious quantities of champagne I knew we would be drinking. I guessed I'd know most of the people there, it was just a shame that none of them had their own children on social speed dial; conversation with someone with vaguely similar interests would have been good.

An essay that I'd left to the last minute meant I was running late. I abandoned the little run-around dad had bought me and did one of those middle-aged-woman trots to the front door, hampered by the pencil skirt and court shoes I'd chosen for this evening. It wasn't my usual attire. I planned to return the skirt at the weekend and the price tag was digging in. I rang the doorbell and stood there, adjusting the pointy bits of cardboard whilst I waited for someone to answer.

Peering through the distorted glass of the door, I could make out the familiar shapes within the hallway. It didn't look like anyone was coming so I rang the bell again, for longer this time and within seconds a body emerged from the kitchen at the end of the hall. Said body then conducted a noisy search for keys. It is claimed that once, five years earlier, in the middle of the afternoon, one of the houses in the road had been entered by a stranger who, while the family enjoyed a BBQ in the back garden, had helped themselves to a carriage clock and a Le Creuset saucepan, and ever since then, my parents have literally lived behind lock and key.

Keys retrieved, the door opened and my dad greeted me with a smile and open arms, his hands like meaty versions of the claw in the arcade game. He placed his hands on my shoulders and pulled me towards him for a peck on the cheek. I could smell cigar smoke; the celebrations must have started without me.

"Hello, love," he said, "you don't need to wait. You should have come straight in."

"I would if I had a key," I mumbled. Despite my frequent visits, neither of them had thought to provide me with one.

"Pop your bag upstairs and come and join us," dad said as he went back down the hall, seemingly in a rush to get back to the party.

On my way upstairs, I passed framed photos of family holidays in Benidorm and Mallorca showing me and my brother as children. As a kid, I was always proud and slightly smug that we could afford to go abroad when my friends' parents could only manage Devon or Cornwall. I loved going back to school, deeply bronzed after days spent on Spanish beaches.

My parents displayed more recent memories in the lounge, thrusting in visitors' faces evidence of my brother's achievements – his graduation, his wedding to the lovely Kate, and more recently, fatherhood to the simply perfect Angus. I was less well represented, having still to achieve anything worthy. Two photos of me had made it to the lounge. One was taken at my twenty-first birthday, dominated by a shiny helium balloon (no doubt to be joined by one similar at my twenty-fifth) and another that captured a moment of laughter at my parents' pearl wedding anniversary last year.

I stood for a moment in the doorway of my room, ready to be transported back to my teens. The emotions of young crushes, the trauma of arguments with friends, the pressure to follow fashion and trends but also to be unique and carefree. Hours poring over magazine problem pages rather than speak to mum about my worries or ask friends whether my body was normal (and risk finding out it wasn't).

My nostalgic reflections were abruptly shattered by an ironing board that stood unapologetically on my faux sheepskin rug and a pile of washing balanced precariously on my Pierrot duvet cover. I dumped my bag on the floor and closed the door behind me.

Back downstairs voices came from the kitchen, mostly my dad's as he held court. My mum didn't take centre stage. She would be replenishing platters of nibbles and filling empty glasses, almost fussing, desperate to make sure that no one was left wanting. I knew before I saw her that she would be scurrying around. Honestly, it made me sad. I knew her to be funny and intelligent but, in this environment, she hid behind a range of hostess duties. My parents' house parties were legendary and although dad was the showman, the success of the evening was all down to her. She just never saw it.

In the past, after a few gins, I'd tried to talk to her about her life in dad's shadow but she would brush away any notion that she was dissatisfied or had more to offer.

"I'm happy," she would say.

"I know you are, mum," I'd reply. "I just think there's more to life than being a wife."

"I'm a mum too," she'd say. "And that is the most important job in my world."

Then I'd hug her and change the subject. I meant well but I had no desire to undermine her life choices by imposing my own modern-day values.

My dad turned at exactly the moment I entered the kitchen and stopped his conversation dead to announce my arrival.

"Here she is! Get her a drink, please love." Mum handed me a glass of fizz (Veuve Clicquot, apparently).

I felt bad that I'd arrived too late for a proper catch-up with her. I was just about to give her a kiss hello and a quick *how are you?* when dad called me over to where the men had gathered at the far end of the conservatory. This was always their spot. Here they could open the door to the garden, which apparently meant they could smoke indoors. Fortunately, it was cigars not cigarettes, but mum would still attack the lingering odour with cans of air freshener in the morning. Dad was never out of bed in time to witness this onslaught so he had no idea how offensive she found the smell and of course, she would never rock the boat and tell him.

"You all know Tilly, don't you?" Dad pushed me forward with a hand on my shoulder. I felt like I was expected to do a turn, like one of those 'Girls in Pearls' out of a Country Life magazine. The men nodded and smiled in greeting, accompanied by a ripple of "Hello… Evening… Hi, Tilly."

"Tilly is at Cambridge University," he continued proudly. I'd given up saying that it wasn't *the* Cambridge University as it didn't seem to make a difference, so now I just smiled whenever he provided this information, which he frequently did.

"Always skint though, these bloody students. How much rent do you need this time?" he laughed. It wasn't malicious but it irked me that I did need more help than my brother had.

"Actually, I'm okay this week, dad," I replied, proud that I didn't need another handout.

"Blimey!" *Playing to the crowd.* "What did you do? Rob a bank?"

"Prostitution, actually." A pause, then a ripple of laughter, some of it less than comfortable.

"Always the joker!" Dad gave me a hefty pat on the back before turning to the men next to him who had started a new conversation.

On that note, I excused myself and went off in search of mum, but instead was intercepted by our neighbour, Brenda. I'd known Brenda for years. Her husband, Brian, and my dad had started the haulage business together.

"I heard what you said back there," she said, sipping her Veuve.

I pleaded innocence. "What do you mean?"

"Having sex for money," Brenda helpfully reminded me.

"Oh, that! That was a joke!" I am a rubbish liar, and I could feel myself blushing.

Brenda seemed not to notice. "You know, there's a lot of money in sex," she said.

"Excuse me?" This was not the direction I had expected this conversation, or this evening, to take.

"Where do you think Brian got the money to buy that first lorry?"

"Bank loan?" I asked, knowing that I'd wasted a guess.

"Me!" I raised my eyebrows and Brenda smiled triumphantly.

I thought I knew how, but I waited for Brenda to offer more information. When further detail was not forthcoming, I said, "What do you mean?"

"Sex! Oldest trade in the world."

I couldn't help but give Brenda the once over.

"Oh, I know I don't look the part now."

No kidding, I thought. "Not exactly," I said as I took in her Windsmoor and pearls.

"Sometimes I wonder which 'me' is in disguise." Brenda sounded wistful and I suspected her outfit was for show, just like mine.

"What do you mean?" I said again. I was too sober for this conversation.

By way of explanation, Brenda took a card from her clutch bag and handed it to me.

Diamond Escorts
Elite Service
Professional and Discreet

The phone number underneath was a mobile one.

Was I more surprised that Brenda was a hooker or that she had business cards in her bag at my parents' drinks party?

"I'm currently recruiting," she said like some sort of direct sales rep.

"Oh, I don't think so," I stammered. I really was too sober for this conversation.

"It took me a while to get my head around it too," she empathised, "but then I started earning."

"Thanks," I slipped the card in my pocket rather than risk making a fuss. "I really need to say hello to mum."

"Of course. Think about it though," Brenda said like it was the most normal job offer ever.

CHAPTER THREE

I'd not been back long from mum and dad's and was happily tucking into a bacon butty when the postman knocked on the door and asked me to sign for an official-looking envelope. Said official-looking envelope contained a bailiff's letter, which I read at the kitchen table, heart pounding. The bacon butty no longer appealed and it loitered beside me, half-eaten.

I couldn't understand why it hadn't been paid. I had direct debits for everything. Or I thought I had. And why hadn't I been told before now? This was six months of non-payment, which according to the letter, I now had a week to sort out. Regardless of the why and the how, right now all I knew for definite was that I didn't have £750 lying around. My overdraft was at its limit, and I'd heard too many student debt horror stories to have a credit card. I picked up the phone to call dad, then remembered I'd proudly announced that I didn't actually need any money.

Thoughts of that evening took me back to my conversation with Brenda. I willed the memory to move on, but it was like it had snagged on a rusty nail in my brain. I found my purse and took out Brenda's card. I glanced at my phone. I looked back at the card then back at the phone. I played out what that phone call might lead to, seesawing between paying off my debt and having sex with some sweaty old man. I thought again about asking my dad.

Decision made, I picked up my phone and dialled the number.

"Hello," a female voice answered.

"Hi, mum. Is dad there please?"

"He's away playing golf. Anything I can do?"

I thought quickly and considered my options. Mum wouldn't have £750. This was a sign from the Universe that I was not supposed to ask dad. At some point, I had to stand on my own two feet. *Sweaty old man.* If I was meant to ask him, dad would have been there. *Sweaty old man.*

"Dad mentioned you had a job now and didn't need help with your rent. He's so proud of you. We both are."

Bollocks.

"Thanks, mum. Yeah, it's about time, hey? Look, it's nothing important. I'll catch him later. Love you."

"Love you, darling."

"Bye." I hung up.

Fuck!

I looked at the clock. 10:30.

Fuck it.

I made my way to the kitchen and took a can of Strongbow from the fridge. I glugged on it until I felt it hit my knees.

I returned to the lounge with my cider and slowly reached for my phone and then Brenda's card. I sat down and took a deep, slow breath in and controlled breath out. I dialled the number.

"Diamond Escorts. How can I help you today?" The voice was husky and seductive.

"Brenda? It's Tilly. From next door, Dave's daughter." I waited for her to respond. I had a sudden urge to shit myself.

"Tilly!" Her usual voice returned. "Well, this *is* a pleasant surprise! How can I help you?"

Like she didn't know.

"Um, I need to earn cash... quick. I just wondered if you had anything going." I sounded like I was asking for an extra waitressing shift.

"Well, I do, as it happens. And he's just right for a beginner."

"Okay." A glimmer of hope that he wouldn't be too old or too sweaty.

"Let's meet for coffee and I'll give you the details. 2 pm okay with you? I'll send you the address."

Swept away by Brenda's efficiency, I agreed and hung up. I had a couple of hours for 'personal admin' that I assumed were essential and routine in this line of work. Was it too late to book a bikini wax?

CHAPTER FOUR

I arrived at the address Brenda had given me and parked my little yellow Corsa in a sea of Porches, Range Rovers, and Teslas. Locking the car door, I distanced myself quickly from my now inferior craft and offered a silent apology. My car was used to standing out, albeit in a student car park it was for its clean interior and lack of dents.

The car park was surrounded by a border of perfectly preened conifers, and I followed a sign directing me to *Reception*. Emerging through a gap in the hedge, I lifted my head to take in what I could only describe as a stately home. A circular gravel driveway swept in front of the building, leading up to and past a central porch so large that it had its own rooftop balcony. This balcony was replicated on the actual roof of the building, behind which was a row of six dormer windows that had likely been servant accommodation, four large chimneys, and a central, flag-less flagpole.

The main building itself had two floors, each punctuated by a series of identical leaded sash windows; eight on the top and seven on the bottom, as the front door took the place of one of them. The precision of the architecture was softened by vivid green ivy that grew randomly between the ground floor windows to the left of the door, and by low bushes in various shades of green, some tipped by fragrant lavender flowers.

I entered through the imposing porch, expecting at any point to be tapped on the shoulder and directed to the side entrance. But no tap came, and I found myself in a large foyer with a reception desk to my right. A well-presented, attractive young woman greeted me with a smile.

"Welcome to The Grange," she said when she saw me. She appeared to have made more effort to come to work than I did for a night out. I approached so that I could speak without being overheard.

"I'm here to see Brenda Jones," I said leaning in.

"Oh, yes, Mrs Jones arrived a moment ago. You'll find her in The Barley Suite, one of our private meeting rooms. It's just through the double doors." The receptionist (Katy, according to her name badge) pointed over my shoulder. "Second door on the left."

Through the double doors, I followed a carpeted hallway. I opened the second door slowly and peeked inside. The sight of Brenda sitting there brought up feelings of regret. I was tempted to leave but was I also a tiny bit excited? Too late, Brenda had seen me.

"Tilly!" Brenda stood as I approached and greeted me with a kiss on each cheek. "Thank you for meeting me here. I thought we could do with some privacy."

At that moment, a waitress entered with a tray of coffee, sparkling water, and a selection of petits fours.

I could get used to this. I took a seat in a high-backed leather chair.

Brenda waited for the waitress to leave. "I'm so pleased you called." She leaned forward and placed a well-manicured hand on my knee. "And it's okay to be nervous."

I exhaled and made a conscious effort to lower my shoulders. I hadn't realised how tense I was. Like when the nurse performing a smear test tells you to 'just relax your legs'.

I took a sip of coffee, selected a yellow petit four and took a delicate bite. Ordinarily, it would have been eaten in one, but it felt appropriate to nibble.

"So, I want to start by explaining about the business," Brenda began. "Not all escort agencies are the same and I pride myself on offering an elite service."

My heart skipped at the word 'escort'. What was I getting into? I took a breath and refocused. Relax, I haven't committed to anything. Just listen. I resisted the urge to take another petit four. How on earth was Brenda resisting them? Focus! I raised my eyes from the cakes to Brenda and made a deliberate effort to concentrate.

"I manage a handful of hand-picked girls whom I match with carefully selected clients. No one comes onto the books without a thorough background check and a face-to-face meeting. Our clients come to me with a need for companionship that they trust me to fulfil. Finding a compatible companion takes time, not to mention luck. Then it takes more time to establish trust. My clients come to me because they don't have the time and don't want to rely on luck. They trust me to provide someone suitable."

"So, we're just companions?"

"Yes. Though the need will differ."

Time for another cake.

"If a client wishes to meet in private it will either be at their own home, that I will have visited, or a hotel that I have agreed to. You will never meet with a client in your own home. You may also be asked to accompany a client to an event, a business trip, or even a holiday." Brenda continued.

"Wow!"

"It can be."

This was sounding too good to be true, and you know what they say…

"What about sex?" I had to ask.

Brenda took a sip of coffee and, finally, a nibble of cake.

"Yes, sex is a possibility. You may find that you have a connection with a client which leads to intimacy. And the client will have paid up front for this eventuality."

"So, it's a choice?" I asked.

Brenda leaned back in her chair. "As you can imagine, I have to be careful how I promote this service. There are certain subtleties which I think we all understand, and which I choose to leave unspecified. When you are offered a client, and you can always decline, it is with the understanding that your time together may culminate in some form of sexual activity."

"Okay."

"As I said earlier, it is important to me that I provide an elite service, and for that my team are well paid."

My ears pricked up. Daddy might be paying but I am still a student.

"An evening is £1000; overnight £1500. £2000 per twenty-four hours."

Where do I sign?

Brenda drank her coffee and waited for me to speak.

"It's tempting," I said. "The money would be good. Dad helps me out, but I'd rather support myself."

Brenda nodded.

"But I'm still not sure."

Brenda took a sip of water and placed the glass down slowly.

"I do understand your resistance." Then she smiled, a twinkle in her eye. "But the fun happens outside of your comfort zone!"

"It's the sex…" I said after a moment. No point denying it.

"I get that," Brenda said. "And that is exactly why I am going to start you off with Edward. Edward is one of my most valued clients and a real gentleman."

"Okay."

"So this would be a dinner at Edward's home. He'll send a car to collect you."

"Sounds lovely."

Brenda continued. "Edward is fifty-three and a retired Savile Row tailor. He is a widower, no children, and loves to travel. And he always smells lovely!" Brenda smiled.

"And that would be £1000?"

"Dinner would be £500. I'll let you decide how much further it goes."

I thought of the bailiff's letter.

"Okay. I'll do it."

"Fantastic," said Brenda. She looked me up and down.

"Now obviously, you'll need to do a spot of shopping."

Charming!

"Student chic really won't do." Her eyes settled on my faithful Converse. "I have an account at Selfridges. Your first outfit is on me."

Less offended.

"When is my…"

"Appointment," Brenda offered.

"Appointment," I repeated.

"Saturday. 7 pm. Your money will be transferred at the end of the evening." Brenda reapplied her lipstick, suggesting she had somewhere else to be and the meeting was over. I stood up.

"Thank you, Brenda." I went to shake her hand. It seemed fitting.

Instead, she ended the meeting with the same two kisses she'd started it with. "Welcome on board," she said. "I have a good feeling about you."

CHAPTER FIVE

The wrap dress disguised and enhanced in all the right places, and I had visions of eyes following me as I walked. I'd spent almost £200 in Selfridges and for once I did not feel I was dressed like a geography teacher. I was even wearing matching underwear, and I was almost sorry that Edward was dinner only. Maybe I'd go out after dinner to find someone who would get to see it.

My phone beeped; it was Brenda:

> 'Edward's car will be with you in 15 minutes.'

My stomach flipped and began to churn. My palms became instantly sweaty. At once the dress felt revealing rather than flattering and my visions changed to those of me tripping up in spectacular Naomi Campbell fashion. Was it too late to cancel? Would I get away with a surprise migraine?

I caught sight of the bailiff's letter and mentally pulled up my (matching) big girl pants. It's just dinner, I reminded myself. Eating and drinking.

A car pulled up outside and the driver stepped out, positioning themselves at the kerbside rear door. I grabbed my bag, took one last look at my (pretty hot) reflection, exhaled, and put on my game face.

As I emerged, the car door was opened. "Good evening, ma'am," said a soft Scottish accent.

"Good evening," I replied. "Thank you."

I climbed into the car and slid along the leather seat.

"We will be arriving at our destination in approximately twenty minutes," the driver informed me before a privacy screen was raised between us. How very formal! I was glad there would be no need for small talk, though listening to that Scottish brogue was no hardship.

Fifteen minutes of steady driving later, we entered Netterton, a village I'd heard of and knew to be expensive and exclusive. It was still light enough to appreciate the quaint cottages, the large village green and the cricket pitch. Bet the locals here don't wake up to empty beer cans and broken bottles.

The car turned right at a set of tall, wrought-iron gates that opened as the car approached, closing again once we had entered. We drove down a stone driveway, passing between tall, regularly spaced trees. The car turned left and stopped. I shrunk down and peered through the car window, my head and eyes scanning from left to right. Edward's home was beautiful, and I found myself open-mouthed as I took in the detail. At either end, the building protruded forward (east and west wings?), one of which had a bay window on the ground floor. I imagined there being a cushioned window seat, ideal for relaxing or reading. I caught a glimpse of the red tiles on the steep roof of the bay window. The windows were made up of smaller, leaded panes, and reminded me of The Grange. My observations were halted when my door was opened by another member of staff who greeted me with equal formality.

"Good evening, ma'am." Another Scottish lilt, this time a woman's voice. "Welcome to Netterton Manor. If you'd like to follow me, Mr Barlow is waiting for you in the drawing room."

I followed the uniformed woman, who I assumed was the housekeeper. She made no attempt at small talk. She pointed out the 'ladies' powder room', keeping her head and eyes facing forward as we passed. Was she used to her employer receiving guests like me? Did she disapprove? Maybe she fancied him herself! A *Lady Chatterley's Lover* type scenario!

I absorbed my surroundings as we made our way through the house, a distraction from the nerves that I couldn't help but feel when I imagined the evening to come. The corridor was wood panelled. Paintings were mounted on alternate panels. Flower-topped, half-moon tables stood under panels without a painting. Eventually, though I'm guessing it was less than a minute, we arrived in a dimly lit room, dominated by a three-piece Chesterfield suite. The windows looked out on to an unfamiliar view, so I guessed we were now at the rear of the house. A gentleman rose to greet me.

"Thank you, Rose. We'll see you in the dining room shortly." Rose nodded and stepped aside so I could enter.

"Tilly, how lovely to meet you," Edward said with a broad smile.

Despite our age difference, I found him attractive. He was dressed in a well-fitting suit, complete with waistcoat and pocket watch, and did indeed smell lovely. About six foot, he was trim and I sensed he was physically fit, the kind of man who might have a home gym. Moving to the attributes by which I judge every man, I was pleased to note full lips and hands of a size that belied the precision of his former career.

"Can I get you a drink?" he asked. "Do you like champagne?"

"That would be lovely," I replied, trying desperately to relax whilst preparing myself to be engaging, funny, intelligent. In other words, good value for money.

"Brenda tells me this is your first time," Edward said, obviously at ease with the nature of this evening's arrangement. He filled two champagne flutes and handed me one.

I didn't think it was worth mentioning my conquest in the night-club toilet, so I nodded, then took a sip.

"Well, in that case, I hope you will have a lovely evening." He smiled and his eyes twinkled.

This really is a lovely home." I'd finally found my tongue. "Have you lived here long?"

"Thirty years. It belonged to my wife's family, and we took it over when we married," Edward explained. "Although twenty of those I have lived here alone. My wife, Margot, died far too young. Cancer."

"Oh, I am so sorry," I said with genuine sympathy.

"It was a long time ago now."

"And you've been alone ever since?"

"In the beginning there were liaisons. But the terms of my inheritance meant that I couldn't re-marry without losing Netterton Manor, so I didn't feel it was fair to lead anyone on." He continued. "But luckily I met Brenda, which helped."

I wondered if Brenda was still 'helping' but didn't want to ask.

"Anyway, enough of this doom and gloom, I promised you a lovely evening and at this rate you'll never want to come back! Shall we go through to the dining room?" He gestured towards the door and placed his hand gently on the small of my back as a gesture that I should go first.

The dining room was a beautiful room with a central chandelier and a long, polished table. Around it were twelve upholstered leather dining chairs, hinting at dinner parties that may have taken place and perhaps still did. I knew there weren't any children, but surely Edward had friends. Two places had been set at the far end at right angles to one another. Cutlery had been set for at least three courses and each setting had four different types of glasses, all crystal. It looked like we were in for quite a feast!

"Allow me," said Edward as he pulled out my chair. I sat down and then he seated himself at the table while yet another member of staff approached the table with a bottle of chilled white wine.

"I hope you don't mind, but I've taken the liberty of pairing the wines with this evening's menu," Edward explained as if I'd be disappointed with the lack of choice. "I am promised that this one will go superbly with our first course."

"No, not at all," I replied, happy to be swept along by the grandeur of the evening. "It all seems wonderful."

Wine poured, another uniformed steward appeared with a platter of glistening seafood to share. Mussels, prawns, oysters, and lemon wedges were arranged in a haphazard manner that had no doubt taken time to perfect. The whole thing looked amazing but even so, the sight of it filled me with dread. This was not a good start to the evening. I could feel my face warming and I shifted in my chair. Next to arrive were two lemon-infused finger bowls. I couldn't even bring myself to make my usual joke about lemon soup.

"Bon appetit!" Edward went to raise his glass. Then he met my eyes and stopped. "What's wrong?"

"Seafood. I'm allergic." I crinkled my face in apology.

"No!" he said, mortified.

"I'm so sorry," I said like I'd done something wrong. "It looks amazing."

"No, I'm sorry!" He covered his face with his hands. "I can't believe I didn't ask."

"It's fine," I began.

"It most certainly isn't! Rose!" he called.

Rose materialised like a telepathic ghost. "Yes, sir."

"Can you please take this away and bring some…" He looked at me. "Pâté? Soup? A salad?"

"Pâté would be great."

With that Rose removed the platter and turned. I immediately felt under pressure to fill the void.

"Do you mind if I nip to the loo while I'm waiting?" I asked, taking the easy way out as I struggled to think of anything witty or interesting to say.

"Of course not," Edward replied, standing to lift my chair out. "Let me show you where it is.

"It's fine," I replied, not wishing to add to my embarrassment. "Rose pointed it out earlier."

Once there I studied myself in the mirror. I closed my eyes and exhaled. Why was I nervous? Edward was being lovely. The seafood was being dealt with. Everything was fine.

"It's going well," I whispered. "And you look fab." I gave myself a reassuring smile and a thumbs up, then made my way back to Edward.

I sat down feeling more confident than when I'd left.

"Okay?" Edward asked.

I nodded and smiled. "Yes, thank you." I was relieved that I meant it.

At that moment Rose returned and placed the new dishes in front of us.

Once more, Edward raised his glass. "Shall we try this again?"

I nodded.

Edward raised his glass a second time. "Bon appetit," he said.

I finally raised my own. "Bon appetit!"

We ate our pâté, which was lovely in spite of it being second choice. I felt comfortable enough to bring up the subject of female companions. "Don't you get lonely, Edward?"

"I'm used to it now, but I simply can't risk losing the Manor. This way I get to enjoy the company of beautiful women risk-free."

It seemed like a sad existence to me, but I decided to not pry further. I changed the subject. "I notice your staff are all Scottish. Is that where you are from as well?"

"No, I grew up in Lincolnshire," he said. "Margot's family were Scottish so it's always been a tradition to have a Scottish staff."

"How did you meet Margot?" I asked.

"I was in London as an apprentice tailor, and she was there for the weekend visiting family. Cousins, I think. We met, fell in love, and Margot spent the next ten years trying to convince her father that I was worthy of her." Edward shook his head.

"Is that why you lose the Manor if you re-marry?" I asked tentatively.

"Exactly. Falling in love again would prove to them that I was only with Margot for her family's money. And I will not give them cause to believe that."

"I didn't mean to upset you," I said, placing my hand on his.

"Not at all," Edward replied, covering my hand with his. "Thank you for taking an interest."

We withdrew our hands as the steward approached to clear the table. On his return, he filled our second glasses with a deep red wine.

"Beef?" I guessed.

"Venison," Edward corrected. "My favourite. I hope you'll like it too."

The conversation turned to me as Edward asked about university and my career aspirations. He tactfully avoided the subject of my newest income stream, and to be fair there were times when I forgot I was working.

After dessert came cheese and port, something I hadn't had before but could definitely get used to.

"How often do you… have company?" I asked, wondering if this was likely to be repeated.

"Once a month or so. Would you like to come back?" This time, he took my hand.

"I think so." It was certainly an improvement on Student Night at Wetherspoons.

Edward raised my hand to his lips and kissed it gently. "Shall we move to the sitting room for coffee?"

"Yes, please."

Edward offered a hand and helped me to my feet. Holding both my hands in his he kissed me on the cheek.

"Thank you. I really am having a lovely time."

"Me too," I replied.

Edward hooked a lock of hair behind my ear and our eyes locked. What was the protocol here? In other circumstances I'd have kissed him, but was that allowed? Unsure, I decided against it.

"You could stay a bit longer if you'd like."

"Stay longer?" I asked. Despite the obvious attraction, I was taken aback by his directness, and my eyes widened.

"Obviously I'd pay extra." As if that was the reason for my reaction.

Suddenly, the evening had gone from *Downton Abbey* to *Indecent Proposal.*

"It's up to you of course," Edward reassured me. "You wouldn't need to stay the night. Kenneth could take you home."

What to do?

1.I definitely found him attractive.

2.This is what I had expected when I'd called Brenda.

3.I think he'd be a good person to have my first paid experience with.

4.It's sex. I've done it before with far worse people.

"I'd love to stay," I said finally.

We drained our cups and Edward suggested we retire. "Rose will show you to your room where you can freshen up. My room is just next door so come in when you're ready."

With that, Rose appeared at the door. "If you'd like to follow me, ma'am," she requested for the second time that evening. I followed her up the stairs, slightly uncomfortable that she was privy to what I was about to do. Rose, however, showed no signs of embarrassment.

"Make yourself at home when you get to your room. You'll find toiletries and a robe that you can use," she explained.

I took that to mean that I should arrive at Edward's door showered and undressed, and was grateful for the subtle advice.

Rose opened the door and entered the room, holding the door while I followed her. Of course, the room had a four-poster bed and floor-length velvet curtains. There was also an internal door that must lead to Edward's room.

"The bathroom is just next door," Rose informed me. Then she left the room, closing the door behind her. Her departure seemed a bit abrupt but then again, *have a good time* might have been worse.

Arranged on the bed was a brand-new satin robe.

Please say I get to keep this.

I undressed and put it on. It glided over my bare skin, and I could barely feel it on. Underneath the bed was a pair of brand-new slippers; a step up from the Crocs I usually wore indoors. Also on the bed was a freshly laundered towel and a selection of upmarket travel-size toiletries. Fleetingly it occurred to me that this was a little too well-prepared, but then I figured that Edward's companions would often be invited to stay. It was a precaution rather than a presumption. I took my toiletries and made my way to the bathroom to freshen up.

Back in my room after a gorgeous power shower and a brush of my teeth, I took a look in the mirror. I had a certain glow, though I wasn't sure whether that was a new-found confidence or the wine. I walked to the adjoining door and gave a knock.

"Come in," Edward said. I opened the door and stepped forward into the unknown.

CHAPTER SIX

Edward stood as I walked towards him, my shoulders back and everything else either pulled in or pushed out. He also wore a satin robe though his was navy blue. It was open slightly, revealing a well-defined chest. His calves were toned, and his feet appeared to have been pedicured. Edward was evidently a man who took good care of himself. The bedside lamps cast an orangey light that created a relaxing atmosphere.

"You look lovely," he said, flicking my hair behind my shoulder. "Are you okay?"

I nodded, surprised at how at ease I was with this new intimacy. I'd never been with anyone older than thirty, and that had seemed risqué at the time. Don't overthink it, I told myself. Just go with it.

Reassured that I was content to proceed, Edward undid the belt of my robe and slid it off my shoulders. It fell to the floor behind me and I stood perfectly still while his eyes moved from my head to my toes and back again. What would he make of my thighs? I'd always wished they were slimmer.

"You really are beautiful," Edward said, running his palms down my arms and resting them on my hips. He dipped his head and took my nipple in his mouth, sucking it gently. I gasped and he stopped again to ask if I was okay.

"Yes," I replied, unused to such tenderness. Lads of my age are still in the nipple-twisting, radio-tuning phase.

Edward undid his belt and shrugged off his own robe. I did a quick appraisal of my own and was not disappointed. It's true what they say about big hands.

Edward held out his hand and led me the short distance to the bed.

"Lie down," he said then walked round to the other side, avoiding the need for any ungainly crawling. The covers had been turned down, but the room was warm enough to lay uncovered. Edward lay down next to me and continued to stroke and kiss my skin, exploring and delighting in me with gentle enthusiasm. It was as if I was the paying customer. Concerned that I should be doing more I moved my hand to 'do my bit' but Edward stopped me.

"Wait," he said. "Let me enjoy you." I enjoyed him enjoying me for several more minutes during which my enjoyment was quite vocal. Enjoyment was another thing that lads in their twenties weren't so well-known for.

Then, quite suddenly, "How do you feel about doggy style?" Edward asked.

What a gentleman! I normally just get thrown into it.

"Fine by me," I replied. He helped me turn over.

Kneeling behind me, Edward took hold of my hips and pulled me towards him, then he entered me slowly and deliciously. He is the gift that just keeps on giving, I thought as he continued to thrust deeply. I enjoyed myself one more time before Edward also climaxed and flopped onto the bed. "Oh, Tilly, I do hope you come again," he said with a smile.

What, now? Then I realised what he meant.

We lay side by side for a while and I could easily have stayed there. Although the offer to stay had been made, I didn't want to burst the bubble of this evening. Breakfast in last night's knickers is never cool, so I kissed Edward on the cheek and told him I was going to go home. He softly grunted his acknowledgement. I smirked. Not so different from a twenty-something-year-old, after all.

Back in my own room, I took another quick shower before leaving. Once dressed, I gathered my things, pausing to look longingly at the satin robe. What was the protocol here? It didn't feel right to take it with me but I wouldn't want it to be thrown away. Instead, I imagined it being placed until next time in a drawer marked, *Tilly*. One of many named drawers. Was there still a drawer marked *Brenda*?

I closed the door quietly behind me and returned to the foyer where Rose was waiting. Don't these people ever sleep?

"Goodnight, ma'am," she said, without expression.

"Goodnight," I said. "Thank you for a lovely evening." I blushed, meaning only to thank her for the 'before' bit.

Outside, the driver opened the car door for me again.

"Thank you, Kenneth," I said.

"Kenny's fine, ma'am. Only my mum and Edward call me Kenneth." He smiled and closed the door behind me.

Again, the privacy screen was raised before we set off back to my humble student terrace. I let my head flop against the back of the seat.

What an evening. From the food (seafood aside) to the sex. But surely, I'd just been lucky? I shouldn't get carried away. No doubt there would be sweaty old men whom I would have to deal with diplomatically. But for now, I allowed myself to relax with a smile.

CHAPTER SEVEN

The next day started with a fuzzy head and a throbbing down below. I remembered the pleasure of the night before and the throb turned to a tingle. I looked at the clock; ten minutes before my alarm. I lay back down. I had just the thing for both.

Finally out of bed and feeling refreshed, I gathered my books for the day's lessons. My phone beeped.

> 'I hear last night went well. Can we meet later? B.'

I sent back a quick reply.

> 'In lessons till 3. Can meet then. Tell me where.'
> 'The Grange. See you just after 3.'

As I was leaving, Charlotte, my roommate called me from the landing.

"Tilly, I need to apologise," she said as she made her way down the stairs.

"Okay," I replied, wondering what she'd broken/eaten.

"I haven't been paying you for the utilities. I thought I had but somehow the payments haven't been coming out. I'm really sorry. It's sorted now but I owe you £260. Here." She handed me a pile of notes, fresh from the cashpoint.

"Oh, thank you." That would explain a lot. I took the money.

"I hope I didn't leave you short."

"No, it's fine. See you later." I gave a little wave as I turned to leave the house. If only she knew!

I had more than enough to cover my debt. I should let Brenda know, really. Then I noticed the time and vowed to call her at break.

Morning break came and went without me making the call. So did lunch. I told myself I needed to get to the library and didn't have time. I definitely wasn't avoiding telling her because I'd just earned £1000 in one evening.

At three o clock, I still hadn't made the phone call so I got in my car and drove to The Grange. I would just have to do it face to face.

In The Snug, Brenda was sat by the fire. She stood as I approached and kissed me on both cheeks. "Tilly darling. Lovely to see you." Her exuberance enveloped me. I felt like a home-coming queen and had no immediate desire to burst the bubble.

The waitress laid the coffee out on our table and Brenda made small talk while she waited for her to leave albeit with a devilish twinkle in her eye. As soon as the coast was clear. Brenda leaned in, smiling broadly.

"I hear last night was a success and Edward asked you to stay. He must have been very impressed, so well done." Despite my imminent retirement, I was proud that I'd gained Brenda's approval.

"It was a lovely evening," I said. "Edward is a real gentleman."

"He is," Brenda replied. "And in the bedroom. How was that?"

What did she want? A thrust-by-thrust account? I decided not. "Better than expected."

"Good. So, on to your next job." Brenda sat up straight, ready to brief me on the details.

I interrupted her. "About that..." Time to burst that bubble.

"Hear me out." She raised her finger as if to hush me. "This is a big one! £1500 for a couple."

"A couple?" £1500 was indeed a big one (I'd retire another day) but I wasn't sure about a threesome.

"Bev and George. Lovely couple. It's her birthday. Always wanted to be with a woman so George is going to treat her. He'll be watching," Brenda explained.

"Sounds like George's birthday treat to me," I joked.

"No doubt he'll have fun too. But no sex for him," she warned.

"Got it. Only thing is, I'm not into girls." Not unless a snog for a dare on a school trip counted.

Brenda shook her head. "You don't have to be. It's acting. And then it isn't." She winked. I guessed that Brenda knew this from experience, and it was mildly reassuring. At least my nerves were normal.

I weighed up the pros and cons, worst-case scenarios and possible outcomes. The prospect was daunting but the money was enticing. And how hard could it be?

"Okay, I'm in," I said finally.

"Good for you." Brenda smiled and seemed genuinely proud that I'd found the courage to give it a go.

I returned her smile, and we took synchronised sips from our coffee cups. *I can do this*. I sat back and enjoyed the nervous excitement as it washed over me.

CHAPTER EIGHT

I'd thought about driving to the hotel, but I was relying on there being something to drink when I got there so I was fidgeting in the back of a taxi instead. The hotel didn't look like the sort of place that rented rooms out by the hour, but I still worried that everyone would know why I was there. I quickly surveyed the empty foyer and approached the reception desk.

"I'm here to meet with Mr and Mrs Smith." I cringed inwardly at the obvious aliases and studied a brochure to avoid further eye contact with Keith, the concierge.

"Ah, yes. Miss Brown? They are expecting you. Room 406." Keith seemed unfazed.

Fuck it. If he didn't care, then neither would I. "Thank you, Keith." I walked with as much purpose as heels on a polished floor would allow.

The lift reached the fourth floor in much less time than I would have liked. Shit, maybe I should have gone via the bar after all. The doors opened onto a generic hotel hallway: patterned carpet, potted plants, a smattering of *do not disturb* signs. Maybe this was that type of hotel!

I followed the arrow on the wall opposite and found 406 with ease. I stood still and quiet in front of it, but then remembered that the lift would likely have announced my arrival anyway. I knocked and the door was opened at a speed that suggested someone had been waiting on the other side.

"Tilly?" George asked.

"Yes. George?" I was keen to establish that I wasn't about to go down on the wrong man's wife.

Identities confirmed, I was welcomed into the hotel room and was relieved to see a bottle chilling in a wine cooler and three glasses poured in anticipation.

"This is my wife, Bev." I shook her hand and the formality made me smile.

"Hi, Bev. Happy birthday!"

She smiled. "Thank you."

George then joined us with a glass of something bubbly. He had an arm in a plaster cast.

"Fell off my bloody bike!" he explained when he saw me looking. He handed me the glass before returning for Bev's. I took a sip that I wished was a gulp and smiled at the couple in front of me. Late forties, I reckoned – then I remembered that this was a big birthday so guessed again at a well-preserved fifty. Both were well-dressed but casual, Bev in wide-legged trousers and a silk blouse; George in trousers and a shirt open at the neck.

"Do you do this often?" *What the fuck?* I'd always found small talk to be more awkward than real conversation.

"Together, no, but I've done it with previous partners," George answered.

Bev grabbed George's hand, looked him in the eyes and smiled broadly. "And now it's my turn. A lifelong fantasy."

"Trust me, you won't be the only one having fun." George winked.

I smiled back but my heart was pounding. *No pressure then.* "Just excuse me one minute," I said.

I headed for the bathroom and closed the door behind me before standing in front of the mirror. I exhaled and fanned my face then looked myself right in the eyes. "You can do this," I said in the quietest of voices. I tried a smile. What is it they say? Fake it until you make it? Still not fully convinced, I used a technique I'd read was good for procrastination. I counted down from five to zero. On zero I grabbed the doorknob and opened the door before I could change my mind again.

"Sorry about that," I said. Thankfully, Bev and George seemed unfazed. "So, shall we get started?" They both grinned expectantly. "George, would you like to take a seat?" George sat, evidently looking forward to what was to follow.

Turning towards Bev, I undid the buttons of her blouse. Her eyes were bright and her breathing increased. I could feel her heart beating as I stroked her breast. I undid the belt of my own dress and opened it, revealing the matching underwear that was, at last, getting an audience. I brought Bev towards me and kissed her. She returned the kiss, more tender than a man's.

So far, so good. This was taking less acting than expected.

We undressed some more, our clothes falling in a pile at our feet. I'd kept my underwear on, but Bev was completely naked. I admired her well-toned physique and made a mental note to start a gym membership.

Bev lay down on the bed and I knelt between her legs. Slowly, I made my way down her body, conscious that I would eventually reach unknown territory. It's okay, I told myself. You have one of those as well. I reached her pussy and hovered, taking in the scent that was familiar and surprisingly erotic.

Behind me, a zip rasped and I guessed that George was about to get involved from the confines of his chair jail.

In my head, I did a quick biology book revision of the female genitalia, body parts that I had intimate knowledge of, albeit not from this angle. I had another mini panic as I found myself over-thinking the task ahead. I was about to touch something that was so familiar and yet so alien. Something that was mine and yet wasn't. I hoped my nerves and resistance weren't obvious. How off-putting would that be?

I gave myself a quick talking to, along the lines of *just get on with it* and did another, albeit silent, countdown. Now past the point of no return, I decided that the best approach would be to start with what I liked and wait for clues. Plan made, I went to work and proceeded to pleasure Bev in a way that I would be pleased to receive. This seemed to do the trick as Bev was soon mewing and moving rhythmically beneath me. Judging by the grunts coming from the chair behind me, George's broken arm was no longer an impediment and he was also enjoying the performance. I felt like a goddamn superhero!

After a little more wriggling and groaning, a joint husband and wife climax rang out amongst a chorus of *oh gods* and *holy fucks*. I extricated myself as they wallowed in their post-orgasmic fug, grabbed my dress, and disappeared into the ensuite.

What a high! Jittery with sexual energy, I removed my underwear and, leaning one-handed on the sink unit, I touched myself to my own silent climax. It didn't take long. It was either that or Keith was getting it in the Left Luggage. Tension relieved, I took a quick shower, then dressed, and returned to the bedroom, inadvertently walking in on Bev and George who had apparently found their second wind. Quietly, I collected the rest of my belongings and left the room.

Downstairs, I contemplated getting a nightcap before heading home, but what if Bev and George had the same idea? Somehow that potential threesome felt more awkward than the one I'd just left, and I'd spent long enough outside of my comfort zone for one evening. I decided instead to get a taxi straight home where I had a bottle waiting in the fridge. Once home and changed into a fluffy dressing gown, I sat with a cold glass of wine and checked my bank balance. £1500 had been deposited an hour ago. My phone beeped:

> 'Good work tonight. I'll be in touch. B.'

She sure didn't waste time getting feedback. I sat back and wondered what the next job might be.

CHAPTER NINE

I arrived at my lesson with seconds to spare and plonked myself down next to Fran. Today, she smelled like coconut. Fran was obsessed with The Body Shop and wore a different body lotion every day. My favourite was Moringa and occasionally she'd humour me by wearing it two days in a row.

I gave her a sniff. "Mmm, you smell like holidays."

Fran raised an eyebrow. "Someone's in a good mood." I wasn't usually this perky until at least three o'clock.

Fran and I had literally bumped into each other at Freshers' Fair. I'd been trying to grab a leaflet from the volleyball stand when Fran had turned around, bumped into me and spilled coffee down my vintage *Magic Roundabout* t-shirt. I was gutted but Fran made it up to me by dragging me off to the Student Union and plying me with pints of snakebite and black. We finally made it back to Halls at one in the morning and, in spite of Fran being closer in age to the general student populous, we'd been firm drinking partners and study buddies ever since.

"You look great," Fran whispered, the lecture now in full flow.

I'd treated myself to a blow-dry and highlights. The hairdresser hadn't even tried to hide her disdain when I told her I usually cut my hair with nail scissors and occasionally treated myself to a Boots box dye.

"And your skin is glowing." I'd also had a facial and splashed out on all the creams the therapist had recommended.

We left the auditorium forty minutes later. "Do you have plans for this weekend?" Fran asked.

I didn't but I wasn't sure if I was supposed to keep my weekends free from now on.

Fran continued. "It's my dad's fortieth and his mates have organised a party for Friday night."

"Forty?" How does that work?

"Yes. He started young." Fran brushed away my astonishment. "He's been low since the divorce, so I want to go but I don't want to go on my own."

"I'm not sure." Ordinarily, I'd have said yes without hesitation. "Can I let you know tomorrow? I think my parents might have something on."

"Sure. But don't take too long or I'll ask someone else," Fran teased.

"Oh, please! No one else is as fun as me!"

"I'm sure I'd find someone! Anyway, I'm starving. Lunch?" Fran nodded her head in the direction of the canteen and raced off at a fast walk.

That evening I messaged Brenda.

> 'Anything for me this weekend? Been invited to a friend's place. Don't want to let you down.'

She responded straight away.

> 'Nothing in this weekend. Enjoy yourself. Speak soon. B.'

I messaged Fran.

> 'Mum and dad not doing anything this weekend so I'm free!'.
> 'Yay! Leave Thursday after lessons?'
> 'Sounds good to me.'
> 'And my brother will be there.'
> 'Mmm.'
> 'Cheeky. See you tomo x'

Thursday morning, I picked up Fran from her student house, her weekend essentials in an old Umbro bag. I had brought the Selfridges dress and it was laid carefully on the back seat in a protective bag.

"New frock?" Fran asked. "You have been splashing out!"

"Dad gave me some money. Thought I'd treat myself." I was sure I'd tell her eventually.

"Ooh, lucky you! Listen, I'll need to run Sunday morning, but should be back mid-morning at the latest." Fran was training for a local marathon and was taking it *very* seriously.

"That's cool. Doubt I'll even be up!"

Fran and I wasted no time once we were released from our final lesson. We drove down the motorway like Thelma and Louise, windows open, music blaring.

"It's so good to get away," Fran enthused. "Tom is having a party and no doubt someone will puke in the bath."

Fran had been late getting a house this year and she'd been stuck with two housemates who seemed to be studying for a BA in drugs and alcohol.

"Are you still looking for somewhere else?" I asked.

"Yes, but mid-term moves are really hard." Fran frowned. "I am literally waiting for someone to die or get kicked out."

"Charlotte might be off to France for six months," I said, remembering a conversation I'd had with her just yesterday. "You could maybe take her room till the end of the year?"

"Ooh, that would be fab!"

We drove the remaining sixty miles or so, chatting about job placements, essays we were working on and life after Uni, and arrived at Fran's dad's just after five.

There was a Corsa-sized space on the driveway. "Ha! Alex will have to park on the road." Sibling rivalry never dies. I thought of my own, oh so capable, brother.

We grabbed our bags from the car. "I'll come back for my dress," I said, not wanting to crease it in my Crackerjack-style efforts to carry everything.

The front door was opened by a smiling man in knee-length shorts and an old Duran Duran t-shirt. Judging by the state of it, he'd had it since they were in the charts the first time. It hung off well-defined pecs, and the lower half of well-formed biceps peeked out from the frayed sleeves. Fran greeted him with a shout, breaking my stare.

"Hi, dad! We made it!"

"Hi, Frannie," he replied, coming out to help us with our bags.

"This is Tilly," Fran said. "She's going to be my wing woman at the party of old people!"

"Old! I'm only bloody forty! Child bride, me," he said to me with a smirk. "Hi, I'm Ryan."

"Hi, there," I said. Oh, my!

Ryan went to take my bag from me, but I was distracted by the study of his toned arms, and I fumbled the handover. Our eyes locked briefly as our hands became awkwardly entwined. Ryan winked and I blushed. I mumbled an apology, then turned sharply to retrieve my dress from the car.

"Good to see someone is making an effort," he said, nodding at my party outfit. "What-e-ver!" Fran replied. "Come on, Tilly, let's dump this lot and I'll introduce you to my local. See you later, loser." Ryan stood to one side, and I walked past trying desperately to feign nonchalance and avoid further bodily contact. Once past, I grabbed hold of the banister and hauled myself up the stairs as fast as my cargo would allow.

Bags dumped, we freshened up with dry shampoo and a squirt of deodorant.

"There's never anyone fit there," Fran said. I put on a tiny bit of lippy just in case.

We ordered pints of lager – snakebite was a no-no in civilised society – and settled down in the corner of the bar.

"Have you lived here long?" I knew very little about Fran's life outside of university.

"All my life. I went to school here. Couldn't wait to leave but now I come back every now and then. Especially since mum left." Fran seemed wistful.

"When did she leave?" I couldn't imagine my mum going anywhere.

"About a year ago. I was away so had no clue how bad things were between them. She didn't even leave to be with anyone. Just said she couldn't stay."

How bad must things be to leave even though you don't know where you're going?

"That must have been awful."

Surprisingly, Fran shrugged but I wasn't sure I believed her nonchalance. "Honestly, I'm more of a daddy's girl."

"But do you still see your mum?" I asked.

"Yeah, but only really Facetime. She moved to Scotland to open a bloody hotel!" Fran finished her lager in one. "Fancy a shot?"

"Okay." I knocked back the half pint I still had left.

She came back with a shot and another pint each. "I think my dad is lonely," she announced. "I should come back more."

"I'm sure he understands. Doesn't he have a girlfriend?"

"I don't think so. Such a waste. I mean, he's a catch – right?"

I nodded. How much enthusiasm was appropriate?

"He'd been with mum since he was seventeen," Fran continued. "She broke his heart."

We never spoke like this at uni and I realised how superficial life there was. Despite the perception of independence and responsibility, I lived in a bubble of faux adulthood, protected by a safety net of parents and tutors. Was that why I was enjoying working for Brenda? For the chance of real independence? The sense that I was stepping into real adulthood? Did it matter?

I returned my focus to Fran. We'd been here an hour and the pub had five other people in it – the post-work crowd. They were all middle-aged men in suits eking out the last moments of independence before returning home to assume the role of hands-on dad, adequate DIYer or doting husband. Fran had been right. Lippy was wasted on this crowd.

"Shall we go back to yours? Order a Chinese? Save ourselves for tomorrow night?" Luckily Fran perked up at this. I had nothing else up my sleeve.

"Yeah, I'll message dad. He can pay!"

Back at the house, we sat around the kitchen table. Fran's brother Alex had arrived and the family resemblance was obvious. Dark hair, chocolate brown eyes and lovely cheekbones. I wasn't sure what their mum had offered but their dad seemed to have it pretty much covered.

"I thought Gemma was coming this weekend," Ryan said.

"She's coming tomorrow by train. She had something on this evening," Alex replied.

Gemma? I looked up from my pork balls.

"Alex's girlfriend," Fran explained, perfectly translating my rapid eye movements.

"You'll love her. You all will," Alex enthused.

"Sorry," Fran mouthed.

"Shh," I mouthed back.

We ate Chinese to the point of 'not really needing that last plateful' and then retired to the lounge for a really enjoyable evening of conversation, family memories (where mum wasn't mentioned but neither was she missing), and sibling banter. Whatever had happened between Ryan and his ex-wife and however lonely he might be, he had a great relationship with his kids. Had this always been the case or had the relationship developed since his wife had deserted him? I couldn't imagine my mum doing anything for herself, let alone leaving her family (who would fill the glasses at dinner parties?) and I kind of admired Fran's mum for having the courage to put herself first.

"Well, this thirty-nine-year-old needs to get his beauty sleep," said Ryan as the clock chimed midnight.

"Me too," said Alex. "I need to be at the station at half nine to meet Gemma."

Fran and I looked at each other. Drinks cabinet or bed? We decided on the latter.

"Us too," Fran said. "I could even squeeze in a run tomorrow morning."

"Good for you, babes. Don't wake me on your way out!" I am so supportive.

"I don't know where she gets it from," Ryan said. "I bloody hate running."

Ryan didn't look like he was a stranger to a free weight or a bench press, but I resisted the urge to say anything for fear I'd sound like a gushing groupie and embarrass myself. Instead, desperate to create a distraction, I grabbed Fran by the hand. "Come on, you. Bedtime!"

"Night," we said in unison, leaving the men to tidy up.

I woke naturally at some time after nine, that leisurely type of wake-up when you have nowhere to go and your time is your own. The single bed opposite mine was empty. Fran must have got up for that run. She was good. I stretched indulgently… then realised I needed a wee. Bugger, I was enjoying that!

Wearing a t-shirt I'd borrowed from Fran and supermarket underwear, I made the dash across the landing to the bathroom. Once done and hearing no movement, I opened the bathroom door and prepared to dash back. Ryan came out of his room at exactly the same moment.

"Oops! Morning," he said. His head remained still but his eyes flicked up and down.

I pulled my t-shirt down, more to hide my rather lacklustre knickers rather than any modesty. "Sorry! 'Scuse me." I hurried back to my room, my heart pounding.

I waited until I heard Ryan go downstairs before grabbing my washbag and returning to the bathroom, this time with my towel around my waist. What is it they say about the horse bolting?

By the time I returned to our room, Fran was back and peeling off her sweaty running kit.

"Ten miles in the bag!" she said. "It's good to run somewhere different. Have you had breakfast yet?"

I shook my head. "Only just got up."

"Cool. There's a fab greasy spoon in town. Fancy a fry-up?"

"Love one."

I waited for Fran to get ready so we could go downstairs together. Ryan was sat on the sofa with a coffee and the paper. He turned to face us, "Morning, ladies. Coffee's brewed if you want one."

He had on another t-shirt that did nothing to hide his assets. I felt the heat rise in my face and was worried that Fran would notice. Worse still, that she'd figure out the cause. I turned quickly and studied the bin collection schedule on the fridge.

"We're off out for brekky," Fran said. "Big, fat fry-up!"

"Lovely," he replied. "I'll be off down the club about two to start setting up. I'm sure you'll be back before then but in case you get side-tracked, that's where I'll be."

"Okay," said Fran. "Do you need any help?"

"Not really. In fact..." He reached into his wallet and pulled out two twenty-pound-notes. "Get something nice done for the party."

"Ah, thanks dad," said Fran.

"Thank you," I said, though I had plenty.

"Right, then. Breakfast then town!" Fran kissed her dad goodbye.

"Bye, Ryan," I said. He had a lovely smile.

Breakfast was just the job for a fuzzy head that wasn't quite a hangover but wasn't quite a 'get out of jail free' card from the night before. Feeling human again, I drained the lukewarm dregs of my tea.

"Where do you want to spend your dad's money?" I asked.

"Um, we could get our nails done?"

"Listen," I began, "my dad already gave me some cash for this weekend. You treat yourself."

"Are you sure? Just for once I'd love to not feel like a grungy student," Fran said.

"Of course." We left the café and made our way to the high street to track down a couple of last-minute hair appointments. Then Fran spotted a charity shop, the Mecca of all students.

"Shall we?" she asked.

I was about to agree when a boutique across the road caught my eye. The frontage was fully glazed with dusky pink woodwork and wrought iron panels at ground level. Each window displayed a chic, headless mannequin. Ornamental trees marked the left and right of the shop front.

I pointed. "What about that one over there?"

"Belle Amie? That is my dream shop. With nightmare price tags!"

"Come on, let's take a look anyway." I grabbed her sleeve and gave it a friendly tug.

"Okay. But don't say I didn't warn you when you fall in love with something you can't afford."

We'll see about that.

Inside the shop, the displays were minimalist. Headless mannequins posed between rails and shelves of clothes in the colours of the season. The shop assistant, a walking advert for a particularly chic ensemble, turned from the trouser display she was titivating.

"Hi, there. Welcome to Belle Amie."

"Thank you." Was she about to pounce? Follow us round like we were on rails? When I was a teenager there was a 'Denim Warehouse' where you couldn't move without a shop assistant tracking your every move.

"Let me know if I can help with anything," she said and turned back to her display. Thankfully not.

Fran and I went our separate ways, each adopting our own particular browsing technique. I preferred the stroke and move on approach, only stopping to study something further when the fabric had passed the touch test. Fran, on the other hand, would hold an item up against her, check the price and then replace it with a look of true remorse.

I spotted the shop assistant. A wicked idea popped into my head, and I smiled to myself as I approached her.

"So, my friend and I have a fortieth birthday this evening and we'd like something suitably stunning and borderline slutty." The Selfridges dress could have a night off.

The shop assistant looked shocked. "I'm not sure…"

"But stunning will do."

She looked relieved. "That I can do."

She looked us both up and down then moved around the shop gathering garments and shoes with a logic that only she understood.

"These are yours," she said, handing me half of the pile. "And these are yours." The remainder went to Fran.

We took our mystery selection and entered the changing rooms, excited to see what the psychic shop assistant had chosen for us.

We emerged from the changing rooms and turned to face one another.

"Wow!" we both said.

Neither of us was wearing anything that we would have chosen for ourselves. The colours, the styles, were all unfamiliar yet absolutely perfect.

Fran's high-waisted trousers accentuated her enviably flat stomach and peachy bum. The dress I'd been given was doing wonders for my bust, and my waist had never looked slimmer.

"We'll take the lot!" I announced.

"Tilly!" Fran exclaimed.

"Shh." I placed a finger to my lips. "We look too good to put this lot back." I handed over my card before she could argue further.

"Thank you so much," said Fran as we left the shop swinging our branded paper bags.

"My pleasure." I steered Fran in the direction of a sign that promised 'walk-ins were welcome'. "Next stop!"

An hour later, washed, blown, straightened, and sprayed, we strutted down the road like Charlie's Angels, catching our reflections in shop windows. We oozed the power of a good haircut!

"Fancy a quick one?" Fran asked as we passed a pub.

Thankfully it was busier than the one last night. "Why not?" It was so good to be away. Good company, a change of scene, and enough money to enjoy ourselves properly.

We ordered two Sauvignon Blancs – these were not pints of lager hairdos!

We got back about half one and Ryan had already left. We grabbed a late-ish lunch of leftover Chinese.

"Should we go and help your dad set up?" I asked.

Fran pulled a face. "I could really do with a powernap before this evening, she Said. "These early morning runs are knackering!"

"Will your dad mind? I do have an essay I could be working on."

"Nah, he'll be cool. He'll be there with all his rugby mates anyway."

I took my laptop and notes from our room and left Fran to sleep. I set myself up at the kitchen table with a view of the back garden, enjoying the peace and quiet.

Almost three hours later, I'd made good progress and was in my own world when the front door opened and Ryan and Alex piled in, laughing about a story that one of Ryan's rugby mates had told them.

"Hi, Tilly," Ryan said. "No Fran?"

"She's having a lie down."

"Sensible." He smiled. "Your hair looks nice."

"Thank you." Did I just blush?

I noticed that Alex was alone. "No girlfriend?"

"Friend emergency." Alex rolled his eyes. "Apparently."

"Oh, that's a shame," I said.

"Her loss." Where had the gushing boyfriend gone?

"I've booked a taxi for seven," Ryan said. "I thought we'd have a glass of something here before we leave."

"Sounds good," I said. "I'll go wake Sleeping Beauty." I gathered my stuff and made my way upstairs.

I knocked gently. "Wakey, wakey." I slowly opened the door.

Fran showed no sign of having heard me. I sat on her bed and stroked her hair. "Coo-ee," I said softly in her ear. She grunted a little *hello*.

"It's nearly half five. Drinks with your dad before we go out. Taxi's booked for seven."

"Mmm." She groaned some more and stretched.

"You want a cup of tea?" I asked.

"Please."

"Coming right up, madam!" I pecked her on the forehead and left her to wake up properly.

By the time I got back upstairs, Fran was sitting up, checking her phone. I handed over the cup of tea.

"Tom's posted photos of the kitchen this morning. Bottles everywhere." She shook her head and showed me.

"I hope he tidies up," I said.

"He won't. The sooner I'm out of there the better."

"I'll speak to Charlotte when we get back. We'll sort something out." I clapped my hands to clear the air and raise the vibration. "Anyway, enough of that – let's get ready to party!"

"Yes!" She sat up straight and issued orders like a Sergeant Major. "I'll quickly drink this then shower in dad's en-suite. You can use the bathroom." I grabbed my stuff and got to work.

Less than an hour later we were washed, shaved, and feeling like a million dollars in our party outfits. Ryan gave a wolf-whistle when he saw us.

"Well, don't you pair scrub up well?" I caught his eye and my stomach fluttered.

He turned to Fran and kissed her on the head. "You look lovely, darling."

Alex looked up briefly, "Yeah, you look okay." Brother code for *you look great.*

Ryan brought over glasses of champagne. "Don't tell the rugby lads!" he whispered.

"Happy birthday, darling daddy," Fran said, raising her glass.

We chinked our glasses. "Cheers."

The taste reminded me of my evening with Edward. Had he been in touch?

Ryan checked his watch, "Taxi should be here soon. Anyone need a wee?"

"Honestly, dad!" Fran shook her head and punched him on the shoulder.

A car horn sounded outside.

"Taxi's here," shouted Alex. "Shotgun!"

Ryan and Fran laughed. "Alex and I would argue every morning on the school run about who was sitting in the front seat," said Fran. "Mum would only give it to the person who was ready first."

Ryan walked on ahead towards the taxi. Alex and Fran exchanged glances.

"Is your dad okay?" I asked.

"He will be. Now come on." She linked her arm in mine and we tottered off down the garden path.

It didn't take long for the party to get into full swing – the rugby lads saw to that. Sometimes we could even hear the disco over their own enthusiastic rendition of each song.

I was at the bar taking a breather from the Jackson Five when Alex came up to me.

"You having fun?" he asked.

"Yes, thank you." He really did have lovely eyes.

"You pulled yet?"

"Not yet." Fran and I had been too busy throwing shapes on the dance floor to suss out the snogging potential.

"You look great, you know," he said. "Not at all like a student."

"Thank you." Where was this leading?

"You want to find somewhere quieter?" he asked.

So that's where. "What about your girlfriend?" I reminded him.

"Not here, is she?" He leaned closer and I inhaled a mix of sweat and lager.

"Alex," I said, removing his hand from my shoulder. "You have a girlfriend."

"But Fran said you fancied me."

"You're not bad, but you have a girlfriend."

I walked away and re-joined Fran who was busy pushing pineapples and shaking the tree. When the DJ started playing songs that didn't come with their own dance moves, we joined the rugby lads for a boat race (or maybe three) and spent the rest of the evening partying like students, even if we didn't look like them.

CHAPTER TEN

I tried to lift my head from my pillow, but it was full of headache. I opened my eyes and flicked them around the room. My dress was in a pile on the floor and there was a lump in the bed opposite that I assumed to be Fran.

I peeked under the covers. Underwear still on. My mouth felt like something had crawled into it and died so I took a sip of the water that somebody (me?) had had the foresight to put by my bed. I had an urgent need for the loo and managed to ease myself out of bed and walk across the landing without meeting anyone this time. Safe in the bathroom, I peed what smelt like neat Apple Sourz then cleaned my teeth twice and gargled with a mouthwash that optimistically promised 'iceberg freshness'. I looked in the mirror. I may have removed my dress, but make-up removal had eluded me. Mascara flakes peppered my cheekbones, so I treated myself to a full cleanse, tone, and moisturise after which I felt slightly less rubbish.

I threw on jogging bottoms and a baggy sweatshirt and went carefully downstairs in search of a strong cup of tea.

"Morning!" Ryan said as I entered the kitchen.

"Fuck!" I blurted out. "Sorry… I didn't expect anyone to be up."

"Couldn't sleep any more," he said. His hair was damp and I caught a waft of freshly-showered man.

I glanced at the clock: 10.30. "What time did we get back?" Did I *want* to fill the gaps?

"About two. You girls went straight to bed." *Good.* "Do you want a cup of tea?"

"Love one." When it arrived I took a sip and the hot, strong liquid performed an ecclesiastical cleansing of my mouth that somehow tasted like dead badger again. 'Iceberg freshness', my arse! I drained the cup and immediately poured another from the pot.

"That was amazing. You want another?" I asked.

"I'm okay for the minute, thanks." I don't think Ryan shared my rapture.

A bedraggled Fran entered the kitchen. "Morning," she groaned.

She looked like I'd felt fifteen minutes earlier and presented me with a mug to fill for her.

"What time did we get home?" she said.

Ryan repeated what he'd told me.

"Oh, my god, those drinking games," Fran said. Flashes of the night before came back to me. *We didn't do anything stupid, did we?* "And you snogged that rugby player!"

"I did what?" I turned quickly from adding milk to Fran's cup. Ryan looked up too.

Fran laughed wickedly. "Psych!"

"You bugger!"

"Oh, babes. I'm sorry. I didn't mean to freak you out." She blew me a kiss and took her tea.

Ryan changed the subject and I said I was going for a shower.

Alex joined us at noon, surprisingly sprightly, and offered to make more tea, which we all accepted. We spent the rest of the day relaxing, though honestly, we weren't capable of much else. There was never really an opportunity for Alex or me to mention last night's conversation and I had no desire to bring it up in front of Fran and Ryan. Every now and then I would look over at him to see if he was trying to catch my eye, maybe to mouth an apology or offer a cheeky wink, but neither were forthcoming. Maybe he didn't remember.

At around three o'clock Ryan opened the fridge and pulled out bottles of cold lager.

"Hair of the dog, anyone?" he said.

Although we shuddered slightly at the first gulp, it wasn't long before we were all on our second bottles.

Dinner was takeaway pizza. While we waited, Alex was dispatched to fetch more beers from the fridge in the garage and Fran popped upstairs to the loo.

Ryan and I sat opposite one another. I recalled our impromptu meeting on the landing and wondered if he'd thought about it since.

"You know I don't normally run around half naked in other people's houses," I teased. "If I'd known you were upstairs, I'd have covered up a bit more."

"Don't worry about it," Ryan replied with a smile. "I didn't see anything you should be ashamed of." I smiled coyly. *Oh my.*

Fran's return saved us from taking this line conversation further and Alex returned with handfuls of beer bottles to a small cheer. We spent a pleasant evening drinking beer and chatting. Ryan described his recent foray into the world of online dating, and I was shocked to hear he'd been unsuccessful.

"They don't know what they're missing," Fran consoled him.

"Yeh, their loss." I added neutrally. *What was wrong with some women?*

"So, what about you girls?" Ryan asked. "Graduation is just around the corner."

"I've narrowed it down to four law firms that I'd be happy to get an offer from," Fran replied. Fran had been researching law firms since our second year. I really hoped she wouldn't be disappointed.

"What about you, Tilly?" Ryan asked.

"Oh, I'll just be happy with a 2:1," I replied. "See where life takes me after that."

"I don't know how you can live like that," Fran spoke, her mouth full of pizza.

Ryan chuckled. "Never been one to live on the edge, have you Frannie?"

"Nothing wrong with a plan," she answered.

"Sounds like you're more of a risk-taker, Tilly." Ryan's eyes settled on mine.

I reflected on my actions over the last few weeks. I nodded. "I guess I must be."

By now our pizza eating had slowed and we'd started to leave the crusts; a sure sign that stomachs were reaching capacity.

"Anyone want more?" Ryan asked.

We all shook our heads and patted full stomachs.

He stood to clear the cardboard boxes away. "Want anything while I'm up? Another beer? Something stronger?"

Fran and Alex both asked for another beer. I decided to quit while I was ahead.

"I'm off to bed," I said. "I'm flagging." Despite a chorus of cries that I should stay, I left the three of them to catch up some more and wasted no time getting into bed. Gotta love an early night.

CHAPTER ELEVEN

I woke with a start. Once I'd worked out where I was, I tried to figure out what had disturbed me. No bad dream lingered and there was no noise coming from within the house or outside. I could make out a shape under Fran's covers. I wondered what time that party finished. I groped around on the floor for my phone and found it on top of my clothes: three am. I needed the loo and wanted a drink. I'd seen lemonade in the fridge so decided to nip downstairs.

I fumbled my t-shirt on and left the bedroom quietly, though judging by the snores, my caution probably wasn't necessary.

Downstairs I was surprised to see a light on in the living room. Ryan was perched on the edge of the sofa, leaning forward with his head in his hands. In front of him were a half-empty bottle and an empty glass. I watched as he refilled the glass with one hand, wiping his eyes with the other. He sniffed and inhaled sharply. Was he crying? At that moment he raised their head and looked in my direction.

It was too late to leave but I wasn't sure I should stay. "Ryan?" I said. My legs carried me forward and I sat down next to him.

"Ryan?" I said again. "Are you okay?"

"I can't do this," he said.

"Do what?" *Should I wake Fran?*

"She left me."

The penny dropped.

"You'll be okay," I said. I put my hand on his shoulder. It took all my willpower not to give it a squeeze.

Stop touching him. I lowered my hand.

"I loved her so much," he said, taking a glug of neat vodka. She really had fucked him up.

"I know." I moved the bottle out of his reach. In the gloom of the room and his mind, he didn't seem to notice.

"You're lovely." He placed his hand on my thigh. My bare thigh. "Thank you."

Ryan looked at me. Well within my personal space. He had great lips. And a hand on my bare thigh. I held his gaze.

That was the point at which I should have removed his hand, replaced his vodka with water, fetched him a blanket, and gone back to bed. That is what I should have done.

Instead, I continued to hold his gaze. His hand travelled ever so slightly up my thigh and I responded by shifting ever so slightly towards him. He leaned in and kissed me on the mouth. Thoughts of what I should do dissipated, and I kissed him back. He put both hands under my arse, lifted me effortlessly from the sofa and sat me firmly on his lap. Despite the vodka he'd consumed and the grief he felt for the loss of his marriage, his body had other ideas. Sitting astride him, his hands travelled up my rib cage, my skin on fire as his thumbs grazed my breasts.

I should have stopped kissing him, stopped grinding my crotch against him, and removed his hands from inside my t-shirt. But the decision-making part of my brain had other ideas. Inappropriate, intoxicating ideas. Then I heard footsteps. I stopped moving immediately and raised my ear slowly to the sound.

"Don't stop," he rasped. Too many body parts were working at the same time to expect his ears to be at their best.

The toilet flushed and the footsteps returned to the room they'd come from. Ryan still wasn't distracted but I stopped kissing his soft, firm lips and reluctantly removed his strong hands from my tingling skin.

"We can't do this," I whispered as I steadied my breathing. "Fran and Alex are upstairs." Because of course, that's why this scenario was utterly wrong. I removed myself carefully and reluctantly from his lap.

Ryan took a moment to collect himself. "I'm sorry," he said. "I shouldn't have done that."

Oh, please don't apologise. "I'd best go back to bed."

I left him with a blanket and went back to bed, without the lemonade.

Back in bed, all my senses were on overdrive. His smell was everywhere, and I worried that Fran would wake up and think he was actually in the room. Where he'd touched me, my skin still burned. My desire was overwhelming, though with Fran in the bed opposite, there was nothing I could do about it.

I must have drifted off eventually. I was woken for the second time, this time by Fran who was shuffling around the room, semi-dressed.

"I'm going for a run," she said. "Twelve miles. Alex is coming on his bike. We won't be long."

"No probs," I said. "I'm sure I'll be fine."

As Fran and Alex left the house, I heard them congratulating themselves on their early morning training session. I lay in bed and reflected on last night's unexpected turn of events. In the clear light of day, I could hardly believe it had happened. Total madness. Utterly wrong. What if we'd been caught? Various body parts were telling me it might have been worth it.

I heard Ryan's bedroom door open and waited to hear movement. Nothing. Not a creak. Not a footstep. My heart started to race.

I knew what I should do. I also knew what I wanted to do. I got out of bed and moved towards the door.

I heard Ryan take a step.

Stay where you are. No – keep walking.

Whilst my brain was considering the rights and wrongs, my hand lifted and opened the door.

I prayed that I looked suitably nonchalant. And that he couldn't smell the pheromones.

"Morning," Ryan said. He looked surprisingly fresh for a man who had been drowning his sorrows in vodka only a few hours before. And surprisingly un-coy. I waited for him to speak. Did he even remember?

"How are you?" he asked. Cool.

"I'm good." Cooler.

"Alex and Fran have gone out." *Fact or question?*

In case it was the latter, I said, "Fran's gone for a run. Alex is on his bike."

"Twelve miles, Fran said." Fact then. "I'm guessing they'll be at least an hour." He took a step backwards into his room.

"I need to clean my teeth."

"Okay."

I walked past and somehow got through the sexually charged forcefield that surrounded him. He waited there while I used the bathroom. I was thankful I'd peed earlier. I opened the door, conscious that this was another point at which I could change the end of this story. Again, my loins told my brain to shut the fuck up and I walked towards him.

I stood in front of him. For a moment we were both motionless. Then he pulled me towards him and there was no going back. His hands were on my waist, then they were travelling upwards, lifting my t-shirt over my head. I stood naked before him, aroused by my own vulnerability and his obvious desire. I felt powerful, and yet I'd done nothing. Ryan removed his own t-shirt and I pushed down his shorts, stealing a quick look at the goods. Oh my!

He lifted me up and I wrapped my thighs around his waist. Pulling me in tight against him, he walked us over to the bed, laid me down and knelt over me on all fours. But I had other ideas.

"Lie down," I instructed. And like a good boy, he did.

He lay on his back and I straddled him, hovering just above his expectant cock. Leaning forward, I kissed him, enjoying the sense of control. As we kissed, I felt his hand between my legs, fingers sliding across my wetness, grazing the sweet spot (another point for the older man), and I whimpered. I was (so fucking) ready.

I lowered myself onto him and basked in the sound of Ryan's groan as I slowly sank lower. We moved together with sweaty abandon, and Ryan came like a man who hadn't for a while. I didn't, but he skilfully took care of that.

After a few minutes, Ryan spoke. "Thank you," he said.

"Thank you?" Surely 'wow' was more appropriate?

"That was amazing. And I fucking needed it." Ryan laughed.

"I aim to please," I said, smiling. "But I need to leave your bed."

Reality bites.

"Yes," Ryan said. "This would probably take some explaining."

I rolled across and kissed him. He kissed me back and I knew that with more time and less risk, there would have been a round two. I picked up my discarded t-shirt and tiptoed back to my room, in spite of there being no-one to hear me. I flopped onto my bed.

Holy fuck! What was I becoming? I gave a satisfied groan and, I suspect, pulled a face like the cat that got the cream. At that moment the front door opened.

"We're back and we have croissants," Fran shouted.

"Be there in a minute," I shouted back.

I dived into the bathroom, a little sad that I would have to wash Ryan off so soon.

Smelling less like sex but still with that post-orgasm floatiness, I dressed and joined Fran and Alex downstairs, as did Ryan.

"You look pleased with yourself," Fran said to her dad.

"I guess being forty suits me," he replied, flashing a triumphant grin.

"Well, whatever it is, do more of it," was Fran's advice.

Ryan and I looked at each other before quickly looking elsewhere.

"So, what's the plan today?" Ryan asked. "Are you all going to desert me?"

"Afraid so, dad," said Alex. "Back to work tomorrow."

"You want to stay another night?" Fran asked me. "Or do you want to get back?"

Monday's lectures had been cancelled due to staff absence and we'd been told to 'use the time wisely'.

"I don't mind staying," I said.

Please let's stay.

"I'm in no hurry to get back to that pigsty of a house," said Fran.

"Well, that's settled then," said Ryan, his eyes bright. "I was going to do a roast… unless anyone fancies a pub lunch."

"Pub lunch," we shouted in enthusiastic unison. With some effort, I managed to suppress a smile, but my stomach did a flip at the prospect of more time with Ryan. Would it happen again? I couldn't help but hope it would.

CHAPTER TWELVE

We arrived at the carvery just after one. Ryan and I sat on the bench seat, Alex and Fran opposite. Ryan's hand rested between us on the seat, his fingers spread, his little finger just grazing my thigh. His touch was like an electric bolt and it made it hard to concentrate.

"What does everyone want to drink?" Alex asked.

We gave him our orders and Fran jumped up to help him carry them back.

They hadn't long left the table when Ryan spoke. "I'm glad you're not leaving today."

"Me too," I said. "What if Fran doesn't need another run?"

"I'm sure we'll think of something." My stomach flipped. The sex and the risk-taking were a heady mix.

Alex and Fran returned with drinks. "We can go up whenever we're ready," Fran said.

Thank goodness. I needed to move before I lost all power of coherent thought and speech.

We ate lunch with a surprisingly normal backdrop of family banter and discussion. A waitress cleared our scraped dessert bowls and Alex looked at his watch.

"I'd better get off," he said. "Shall I run you all home?"

Home was a couple of miles away. I decided the fresh air would do me good.

"I'll walk, I think. I need it after this weekend!"

"Sounds like a good idea," Ryan said

I looked at him, eyes wide. Think startled deer.

"I'll be fine," I said.

Seriously? Might as well wear a placard. I glanced at Fran who was checking her phone, apparently oblivious to any hidden agenda.

"I know. But I'm forty now – need to watch out for that middle-aged spread." He grabbed hold of his taut stomach and feigned a wobble.

"I think you're safe for now," I said, resisting the urge to run my finger down his six-pack.

"Best not get complacent though, Pops." Fran punched him in said taut stomach. "I'll get a lift, Alex. These legs need a rest!"

Alex said goodbye to us all and Fran jumped in the car with him. "See you at home," she shouted over her shoulder.

"Well," said Ryan.

"Well," I said. Well, indeed.

"Come on, I'll take you home the pretty way." Ryan indicated the direction and I followed.

We walked down the path in a silence that was deafening, and it was a relief when Ryan finally spoke.

"I hope you don't think I normally prey on my daughter's friends."

Did I? No. This was not like when our sixth-form teacher sent dodgy texts to Laura Dodds.

"I don't," I said.

"Good. Because…"

"It's okay," I said. Did it need explaining? Couldn't it just *be?* "I've had fun."

"Me too," he said. "And you're okay with fun?"

"Ryan, I'm twenty-three. I'm totally okay with fun."

"Good."

We turned into a narrow track that could easily have been missed were it not marked by a public footpath sign.

"Down here," Ryan said. "I'll show you where I used to smoke tabs as a teenager!"

The track led to a wooded spinney. We passed a dog walker and greeted each other.

"Did you know them?" I asked.

"No. Come on. Not much further."

Well, if he wasn't worried about being seen… I decided to go with it and enjoy whatever he had in mind.

At a large oak, we turned off the track and made our way through the trees. After a hundred metres or so we came out into a clearing with a shed-sized shelter.

"It's a bird-watching hide," Ryan said. "Not sure it's been used by many bird watchers though."

I imagined the various non-bird-watching activities that might have gone on over the years.

Once inside, I was surprised at how well-maintained it was. It was essentially a garden shed with a horizontal hatch and a narrow shelf in two of the four walls. As you'd expect there were a few cobwebs and empty beer cans, but thankfully, it didn't smell. On one of the shelves was a damp-looking book entitled *UK Birds*, left by one of the few legitimate users. Ryan shut the door and bolted it behind us.

"You like?" he asked.

"Very cosy," I said smiling.

"Not too grim?" he asked.

"For bird watching?" I teased. "No, it's spot on."

"Forgot my binos, I'm afraid," he said, moving towards me.

Enough verbal foreplay.

Ryan placed his hands firmly on my hips and held my gaze. He kissed me, then stopped, again holding my gaze. Slowly, he sank to his knees, lifted my skirt and kissed me through my underwear. He ran his finger around the seam and eventually did things with his tongue that I could only have hoped for. Afterwards, he held me as I savoured the glow of a most magnificent orgasm, which was handy as my legs were momentarily useless.

How do I follow that? I opted for a hand job but Ryan stopped me.

"We need to get back," he said.

"But what about you?" I asked.

He paused. "You're right. There's no way I'm going outside with this bad boy." We both looked down at the 'bad boy' in question.

He spun me around and eased my legs apart, then entered me in one hard thrust, holding my arms above my head. The sex was desperate and uninhibited. A last hoorah, fuelled by the freedom of our environment. Ryan came loudly and continued to move inside me until he could no longer bear it.

"Holy Fuck!"

Now that was a better response.

"I don't think I can move," he said.

"We really need to get going now though," I said.

We adjusted clothing and readied ourselves to leave the hide. Ryan unlocked the door and took a quick look around.

"All clear," he said like some sort of super spy.

We left the spinney and walked the rest of the way to the house, trying our best to act like two people who hadn't just fucked like animals in a shed in the woods in the middle of the day.

Back at the house, Alex had left and Fran was reading. She turned as we came in the front door.

"You two took your time," she said.

Fuck!

"Oh my god!" Fran said. "You didn't?"

Fuck, fuck!

"You showed her your old smoking haunt, didn't you?"

Thank fuck!

"Guilty." Ryan raised his hands in surrender.

We exchanged glances.

"Dad, you are so sad!" Fran said with a laugh. "He loves that bloody place, Tilly. I hope you were suitably impressed."

"Oh, I think I made all the right noises," I said.

Ryan had to be at work the next morning so we said our goodbyes that evening as we went up to bed. Fran said goodbye first and then raced upstairs to the loo, leaving me and Ryan alone.

"This weekend was amazing," Ryan said.

Go me! I felt like doing a little jig.

"And it's the first time since…"

Serious face back on. Sombre nodding. Reassuring arm on really fucking solid bicep.

"It was amazing," I agreed. "And I'm glad it helped."

We moved where we couldn't be seen from upstairs and had a proper, no-sex snog. The type of snog that you can put your heart and soul into because it's going no further. For once it has centre stage. For once, it's not a prelude, but the whole shebang.

The toilet flushed. I felt like our whole encounter was based around a series of fortuitous trips to the bathroom. I held his face in my hands and gave him a final peck on the lips.

"Take care," I said. "You're fucking amazing." I left him standing there, forcing myself to climb the stairs, knowing that at any point I could have turned around. Maybe I'd pay him a visit later.

Fran was in bed reading when I got to our room.

"Have you had a good weekend?" Fran asked.

"Really good," I said. "So good to get away."

"You and my dad got on well." I studied her face. I could feel myself blushing. "I really don't want the detail, that might be weird." Fran pulled a face. "But he seems happier."

Despite Fran's apparent acceptance of what may or may not have occurred I was glad when she turned off her light and turned to face the wall.

"Night, babes," she said.

"Night," I replied. Maybe I wouldn't be visiting Ryan later after all. I turned off my own light and sank down under the duvet.

As expected, Ryan was gone when we woke up in the morning and his absence was tangible. I was one step closer to 'normality', like Cinderella when the clock strikes midnight. Fran and I packed efficiently and wordlessly.

"About your dad," I began.

"Honestly, hun, I'd rather not." Fran stopped packing and turned to face me. "I don't know what happened exactly, and I don't want to, but you seemed close. And he seemed happy. And that's all I want to think about."

"Okay," I said. "Thank you."

"Don't thank me, babes. He's a big boy now."

Yup.

"And he can do what he wants with whomever he wants if it helps him get over my bloody mum." She leaned forward and squeezed my hand. "Now let's get out of here and back to real life."

"Real life," I said. "How depressing."

"Not forever though, babes," said Fran. "Six months and we'll be baby lawyers in the big wide world."

I pondered Fran's prediction and was shocked to realise that it was no longer the exciting prospect it had once been.

CHAPTER THIRTEEN

On the drive home, Fran chatted about the law firms she planned to approach for employment. I listened attentively, relieved that there was no further mention of her dad, his new-found smile, or how it got there.

Parked outside Fran's house I waited in the car as she grabbed her bags from the boot. I wound down the window and wished her luck. She crossed herself.

"Don't forget to ask Charlotte when she's moving out," she said, her hands in prayer.

"I won't," I said. "See you tomorrow."

Fran blew me a kiss, picked up her stuff, and turned to enter her house. I wondered what state she'd find inside.

When I got home Charlotte was lying on the sofa reading a text-book with some auction-based TV programme on in the background.

"Did you have a good weekend?" she asked, putting the suntanned presenter on mute.

"Brilliant, thank you." I was momentarily distracted by a variety of X-rated memories. "Just what I needed."

"That's good. Listen, I've got the placement in Paris." She put her thumbs up.

"Oh, that's great news. Well done!" Fran would be pleased. "For how long?"

"The rest of the school year, so only six months," Charlotte answered. Her smile dropped and she stood to face me. "I'm sorry if that leaves you in the lurch with the rent and stuff," she said.

"What? Oh no, don't worry. In fact, I was going to ask if my friend Fran could take your room while you're away. Her housemates are awful."

"Oh, that would be amazing!" Charlotte perked up. "That would make me feel so much better."

"Fab," I said. "I'll call her and let her know. We'll have her round for dinner so we can discuss the details."

"Brilliant. Thanks, Tilly."

Charlotte went back to watching TV and I ran upstairs to call Fran with the good news.

As expected, Fran was ecstatic.

"I will start packing this very minute," she said.

Fran moved in two weeks later and we celebrated with a bottle of wine and a takeaway.

"I'll go halves with you as soon as my allowance comes in," Fran said as we ate.

"My treat," I said, my mouth full of prawn cracker.

"If you're sure," she said. "And you'll have my rent as soon as I've got my deposit back from the old place."

"There's really no rush," I said. I'd seen Edward twice since getting back from Fran's dad's and my bank account was looking healthier than ever.

"That's really kind," said Fran. "Has your dad been flashing the cash again?"

"Yeah, that's right. He thinks I can't cope on my own."

Was I being too generous? I might have to fake a lottery win!

It was Friday morning and Fran and I were having breakfast, actually sat at the table rather than eating toast and marmite in the car.

"This is so nice," Fran said, still scarred by the experience of her previous housemates.

"It is," I said with a sigh. "I'm glad it's worked out."

Fran looked up sharply with a frown. "Did you think it wouldn't?"

"Well, you never know, do you? You can spend too much time together."

"True," Fran reflected. "My sister shared with her boyfriend. They lasted a week."

At that moment the post arrived, and I was happy for the distraction. I came back waving two letters. Formal offers from one of the many law firms we'd applied to.

"They're here!" I said.

"Oh, my god!" Fran thrust her hands forward. "Gimme, gimme, gimme!"

I handed hers over and we wasted no time ripping them open.

"Harper Freeman," she said with a fist pump. "Who did you get?"

"Lloyd, Farmer and Jones," I replied, knowing it had been higher up on Fran's wish list.

"Oh," Fran's joy faded for a moment but returned just as quickly. "We must celebrate!"

"Yes!" I said.

"Tonight?"

"I can't." I'd had a text earlier from Brenda asking if I was free to see Edward. "I've got something on. Tomorrow?"

"What are you up to this evening?" Fran asked with a wry smile. "Is it a date?"

"Yes." Not strictly a lie. "It'll probably be rubbish, but I thought it was time I got back out there."

"After Stinky Jed?"

"After Stinky Jed."

"Well, good for you." Fran patted me on the shoulder. "Tomorrow it is then. Can you pick somewhere we can dress up? You know all the good places."

"Of course." Then I turned and ran upstairs. I shut my bedroom door and sat on my bed to check for messages. I smiled as I saw a new one from Brenda.

> 'Car will pick you up at 7. B.'

I typed back, 'Thank you.' Then I did a little dance before heading back downstairs.

"Penny for them," Fran said as we queued for lunch later.

Huh?" I shook myself at the sound of Fran's voice. "What did you say?"

"I said, 'Penny for them,'" she repeated. "You're awfully distracted today."

"Am I?"

"Yes!" Fran said with a smile. "It's your date, isn't it? You're really looking forward to it, aren't you?"

"I really am." I couldn't lie. A smile crept across my face and refused to leave. "I guess it means more to me than I realised."

"Ah, bless you. I'm pleased." Fran threw her arm around me and squeezed. "I hope it goes well. You deserve someone nice. And clean."

I'd only seen Edward three times and yet it felt more like a relationship than work. Knowing his history with Brenda, I hadn't dared let on that I felt that way and I had no one else to ask for advice. Was this a rookie prostitute error? Was it normal or should I back off? All I did know was that it was a most pleasant way to spend an evening and the money was a bonus.

"Thank you," I said. She may not have known what she was endorsing, but I was pleased that Fran approved of the result. If something makes you feel good, does it matter if the details are a little messy?

I had hoped that Fran would be out when the car came to collect me. Tinder dates aren't renowned for chauffeur-driven Bentleys so I hoped she wouldn't suspect anything. As it was, she was so excited for me that I felt bad for lying.

"OMG! Look at that car!" Fran squealed as the car pulled up in front of the house.

"Really?"

"And there's a chauffeur! Jeez, I need to use your dating site!"

Oh, if only she knew.

"Just a lucky swipe, I guess." I need to get out of here. "I'd best not keep him waiting." I ran out of the house before my acting skills reached their glass ceiling.

"Evening, Kenny," I said.

"Evening, ma'am, are you well?" He tugged on the peak of his cap.

"I will be," I quickly got into the car, relaxing only when the door was closed behind me. Fran was still at the lounge window, waving frantically, eyes and mouth wide open.

As we arrived outside Netterton Manor, I was pleased and surprised to see Edward waiting there. He opened the car door himself.

"It is so good to see you," he said, holding my hand for me to step out of the car. He kissed me on each cheek and I felt the familiar attraction. "Forgive me, but I had to come to meet you myself. Rose was most put out!"

"It's lovely to see you too," I said. "Though it has only been a week."

"Felt like more," he said, leading me inside.

Dinner was the same lavish affair that I had come to expect of my evenings with Edward; the food was amazing, the wines were perfectly selected, and the company was attentive and charming. After an exquisite main course, we took some time before dessert. Edward was stroking my thigh through the thin material of my dress. I was in heaven.

"Have you told anyone about our… arrangement?" he asked.

God, no!

"No," I replied

"You know, what you're doing is very special. It's nothing to be ashamed of."

"I suppose so. I'm just not sure my friends and family would understand."

"As you wish. You are here and that is all that matters to me." He scooped the hair from my neck and kissed me gently.

"I'm not sure I care for dessert," he said. "Shall we retire upstairs?"

"I'd like that," I said. An evening of thigh stroking and neck kissing had left me more than ready to skip pudding.

Edward stood and offered his hand, which I took. I kept hold of it as we left the room.

"Thank you, Rose. We're going to skip dessert and retire early. May we have a bottle of the '99 Dom Perignon?"

"Of course, sir," said Rose, who had appeared silently at the door. As ever, her face was unreadable.

We walked silently up the stairs, turning right onto the landing. Edward pulled me towards him and kissed me. His hands travelled urgently around my body and the kiss threatened to turn into something that I'd rather we did behind closed doors.

"Shall we take this to your room?" I asked, amused but also flattered by his enthusiasm.

"Yes. Sorry. Come straight in. I can't wait."

"I'd noticed," I said with a cheeky grin and a glint in my eye that only seemed to encourage him.

Once inside he undressed me urgently and within a minute, I was naked before him. He undid his own trousers, letting them fall to his ankles and stood proud before me. He took a moment to take me in, his regard hungry. No longer the restrained gentleman, this was a man in the grip of his most basic desire. I was the cause and I owned it. I held his eye.

"Fuck," he said as he turned me to face the bed. I bent over, my hands on the mattress.

With one hand on my lower back, he used the other to guide himself into me. I pushed my hips backwards and gasped as he thrust slowly and deeply. He turned me round. I lay on the bed and lifted my knees high. He pushed them gently apart and licked me, long and slow. I gasped in anticipation, but he was not to be distracted. He mounted me and found his rhythm quickly, his eyes closed, his breathing heavy. When he came he was loud and shameless. He collapsed onto the bed beside me.

"How do you do that?" he said then was still and silent for several minutes. I wasn't aware I'd done much.

I kissed him before leaving the bed. Proud and naked, I walked across the room to retrieve the champagne that Rose must have delivered whilst we were distracted on the landing. Perhaps there were back stairs somewhere? I'd given up trying to figure out how Rose knew exactly where to be and when. Timely and discreet champagne delivery was simply one of her many talents. I poured us both a glass, then returned to the bed and sat down. Edward rolled onto his side and reached for his.

"I don't know how you do it, but it has never been like this with anyone," he said, taking a sip.

Lost for words, I smiled and kissed him. "I aim to please."

"Oh, you do more than that," he replied, before taking both of our glasses and placing them on his bedside table. He lay me down again and returned to the scene of his last lick. It did not take him long to finish what he started, then it was my turn for a long, luxurious orgasm.

"Will you stay the night?" he asked.

I was forced back to my reality. "Can I be home by eight?"

"Of course."

"In which case, I would love to." I drained my glass purposefully.

"I will let Kenny know," he said. "Are you ready for some dessert now?"

"I feel like I've already had it," I said with a twinkle in my eye. "But yes, I'll have seconds."

The morning sun lightened the curtains and there was a knock on the door. Edward was still sleeping lightly, so I wrapped myself in a blanket to see who it was. Stood there was Rose with a Tesco bag, which she handed over.

"For the journey home," she said, then left.

"Thank you, Rose." I smiled quizzically and closed the door. I pulled out a sweatshirt and matching bottoms.

I took the adjoining door to my own suite. I picked up the wash kit and robe that had been placed, as usual, on my bed (not sure why I had my own bed) and went for a shower.

Once dressed, I could hear that Edward was up, so I joined him in his own room.

"Well, don't you look lovely," he said, admiring my new attire.

"Rose's idea."

He nodded in acknowledgement. "Time for a quick coffee before you leave me?"

We enjoyed coffee and freshly baked croissants in his sun-drenched kitchen and then it was time for me to leave. Not for the first time, the return to reality was a wrench.

He kissed me on the cheek, more formal and less rampant than the night before.

"I'll see you again soon?" he asked.

"Of course," I replied. "I look forward to it." I really did.

CHAPTER FOURTEEN

I jumped out of the car and almost took out the postman.

"Morning," he said with a smile. "Nice wheels."

"Morning and thank you," I replied with a grin.

Fran and I had often joked about people doing 'the walk of shame' when we'd seen them bare-footed and winding their way home in last night's silver sequins. Thankfully, Rose's quick thinking had saved me from membership of that particularly unpopular club and I walked confidently to the front door, smug in the belief that grey marl was an invisibility cloak over the figure of my nocturnal activity.

The door was opened by an open-mouthed housemate.

"You stayed the night!" Fran was aghast. "You dirty stop out! Did you…?"

"Maybe."

"Maybe, my arse! How was it?"

"Pretty amazing." Thank goodness I didn't have to lie about everything.

"I just need to get changed," I said.

"Thank goodness," Fran said with a smirk and a top to toe appraisal.

In the car, Fran squeezed me for more information.

"Well, what's he like? Apart from good in bed, I mean!"

"He was very respectful." Easier to stick to the truth wherever possible.

"Is he fit?"

"Yes."

"Good kisser?"

"Yes."

"Do you like him?"

"Yes."

"Will you see him again?"

"Yes."

"Where does he live?"

"With his parents."

"His parents?"

"Yes, but the house is massive. I think they're quite rich." Back on track again.

"Wow, sounds amazing. Anyway, where are we going tonight?"

I had obviously given Fran enough intelligence to be going on with. And I was relieved to change the subject.

"Jago's."

Jago's was a well-known sushi bar and had long been on our wish list.

"I can't afford to go there!" Fran exclaimed.

"That's okay. My treat. Dad won on the Premium Bonds and decided to share."

Once again Fran appeared to believe me.

"Well, if you're sure, that would be amazing! Thank you."

"Absolutely, we are celebrating after all."

The table was booked for seven so I booked a taxi to pick us up at six. In the intervening forty minutes, we went for cocktails in the bar next door and sat sipping Cosmopolitans with a great view of the clientele, a mixture of the smart post-work crowd and the funky pre-night out bunch. The atmosphere was relaxed and sophisticated.

"This is the life," I said, leaning back in the armchair.

"Isn't it just," Fran replied. "Can't wait until we can afford to do this all the time."

I opened my mouth to speak but closed it again. Maybe later.

The restaurant totally lived up to its reputation. It was a pleasure to be served by such attentive staff and the delicious food was beautifully presented. We ate slowly and savoured every mouthful.

"Oh, my god!" Fran exulted. "This is divine."

I nodded in agreement, my mouth full of raw tuna. Wordlessly I asked the waiter for another bottle of champagne.

"Steady, Tilly," said Fran. "This is going to cost a bomb!"

The champagne arrived and I waited for our glasses to be topped up.

"Fran, I need… no, I want to tell you something." I could feel my heart beating. I took a gulp of champagne in preparation.

"Oh my god, what?" Fran was wide-eyed and evidently expecting the worst. "You're not pregnant, are you?"

"No, god no!" I cringed at the thought. "I want to tell you where my money has been coming from."

She opened her mouth to offer an explanation.

"It's not my dad," I said, stopping her dead.

"Oh…" She put down her chopsticks.

I took a deep breath. Where to start? With the nightclub? With Brenda? With being able to pay the bills and treat myself without needing to ask my dad? With the great sex? With the service to humankind?

Fran jumped in before I could decide. "You've been lap dancing?"

"No."

"Gambling?"

"No."

"I know." She raised her hands to halt any incoming clues. "Don't tell me, you're a prozzie."

She laughed. Then she looked at me and stopped.

"What the fuck, Tilly?"

"No, I am not a prozzie," I said.

"Thank goodness. You had me worried then!"

"I am an escort."

"That's the same thing!"

I shook my head. "It isn't."

"Do you have sex?"

"Sometimes." I doubted any jobs would be purely platonic. It would certainly be unexpected.

"Well, then. It's the same thing!"

"It's not. And when I do, it's more than sex. I'm providing a service. Clients need someone like me." I desperately wanted her to understand what I was doing, how it felt.

"You are fucking delusional." Fran leaned in, desperate to not be heard. "You are… *we* are going to be lawyers."

"But that's the thing. I don't know if I want it anymore."

And with that bombshell, I took full advantage of her stunned silence.

"You don't know what it's like. You are the apple of your dad's eye. I live in my brother's shadow, and I can't do anything without my dad having to put his hand in his pocket. And now, finally, I am doing something on my own. I am responsible for me. I don't have to ask for anything." I prepared to bang in the final nail. "And I enjoy it."

"Oh, for fuck's sake!" Fran shoved her chair back and walked off in the direction of the toilets.

I took a well-earned drink and exhaled. The other diners seemed not to have noticed our little difference of opinion.

Fran came back and gathered her things. Her movements were deliberate as if she'd used her time away from the table to plan a swift exit. She spoke in a controlled, almost whisper. "I think it's best if I leave. I don't want to say anything I'll regret."

"Fran, wait!" I called after her with less caution, but she was already heading for the door. The couple on the next table both looked up and smiled sympathetically. They probably thought it was a lovers' tiff. I grabbed the half-finished bottle of champagne and followed her.

"I need to go," I said to the member of staff behind the bar. He quickly prepared the bill which I paid without even looking at the total. "Thank you. It was lovely."

Outside, Fran was on her phone in a doorway opposite. She hung up and watched me as I approached her. Lips pursed, arms folded.

"I just can't take this in," she said. "My head is spinning."

"I do understand," I said.

"I don't think you do," Fran replied. "What if someone found out? You think LFJ would keep you on if this got out?"

"How would they find out?" I asked. "I've only told you and no one else at LFJ knows me yet."

"Have you any idea how tough it is to get into LFJ? There are people just waiting to take your place."

"Like you?" I said, then immediately felt bad, but this was not the time for apologies, In any case, Fran seemed oblivious to the implication.

"You have to think seriously about your future. Be realistic."

"I am being realistic." I was determined to defend myself. "You can't see it, but I am actually helping people. Lonely people. It's not how you imagine it."

Fran looked at me, her eyes narrowed.

"Is that what my dad was? A lonely person?"

"No! For fuck's sake, Fran. Don't be such a bitch."

"And the other night. That wasn't a Tinder date, was it?" She was on a roll now.

"No, it wasn't." I looked her in the eye. "I hated lying to you, but I had to."

"So now you have morals!"

Just then Fran's taxi arrived, saving us from any further mud-slinging.

"Take the cab," Fran said. "I'm not going back yet." She turned sharply and marched off before I could change her mind.

I watched Fran as she disappeared down the road. Should I follow her? Would she be okay?

"You getting in, love?" the taxi driver shouted through the window.

"Yes," I replied, deciding 'no I shouldn't follow her', 'yes, she would be okay', topped off with a defiant dollop of 'who cares anyway'.

Back at the house, I went up to my room, sat on my bed and drank the remainder of the champagne straight from the bottle. Fran had said one thing that I couldn't dispute. I did need to think about my future, and I did need to be realistic. We were due to graduate in a couple of weeks, and I was starting work two weeks after that. And if I was being honest, over the past few months my vision of a career in law had turned from a scene in *Suits* to one in *The Office*.

Despite my initial reservations, I was enjoying my new lifestyle; the part-time hours, the financial advantages, the experiences that I could now afford. I'd done a quick Google search of *trainee solicitors' salaries* and had quickly realised that it would be some time before a career in law would offer me such freedoms. Was I willing to take a step backwards, however respectable that step might be? Was I delusional? Was this new life sustainable? Would I know unless I tried? What if people did find out?

I went to take another swig and realised the bottle was empty. I turned off the light and lay down, fully clothed but too confused and angry to care. I heard the front door open followed by Fran giggling. Then a deep voice. Fran was home and she wasn't alone. I put in my headphones and chose an album that would cover the noise of anything that Fran had planned.

CHAPTER FIFTEEN

In bed the next morning, I replayed the argument with Fran. Was my secret safe with her? Anxiety bubbled up at the thought that it might not be, but before it could take hold, I heard laughter coming from her room and I was jolted back to the present. I shook my head in disbelief. So, she can get pissed, bring a total stranger into my home, no doubt fuck him AND let him stay the night and yet I can't have sex with someone who's actually been vetted, at no inconvenience or risk to her, just because money is involved? The fucking irony! Did she even realise what a hypocrite she was? Probably fucking not!

I was getting twitchy with frustration so was grateful when my phone rang, distracting me. I closed my eyes and took a deep breath before answering.

"Fancy dinner tonight darling?" My mum's voice. "Your brother is down this way for work and he's staying with us."

"Ummm."

An evening of point-scoring and sister-baiting at mum and dad's or one here avoiding Fran?

"Love to. What time?"

"See you at seven? No need to bring anything." She doesn't think I can afford it.

"I look forward to it," I said, with less enthusiasm than the last time I'd said it.

At least this time I could dress in clothes that I liked, and owned, and would keep. I had chosen something classic with a youthful edge (or rather the personal shopper had). I still had to wait for the door to be opened though; still no key and, in suburbia, security still wasn't a dirty word.

I entered the kitchen and managed to side-step my brother to make a quick detour to the utility room and the wine fridge. When I returned, however, he grabbed me in an awkward display of brotherly love.

"Hey, little sis!" He rubbed the top of my head fiercely with his knuckle, then took a step back. "Blimey! Where did the student go?"

Over the past few months my wardrobe and self-care regime had improved, and I'd grown used to it. I liked the feel of a good haircut and quality face cream, and I liked good clothes, especially ones that hadn't been found by chance during a charity shop rummage.

"Thought I'd best make an effort seeing as the prodigal son would be here," I said, punching him on the arm because I couldn't reach high enough for the knuckle rub.

Thankfully, the sibling theatrics were interrupted by mum who, ever the hostess even when it was just us, brought over two glasses of prosecco.

"Thanks, mum," I said, giving her a kiss on the cheek. "I know you said not to, but I brought something. I've popped it in the wine fridge, so it doesn't get warm."

"Thank you, darling. But you shouldn't have. You know how fussy your dad can be."

I smiled. He would not be disappointed.

At that moment, my fussy dad entered the room from the utility, my recently deposited bottle in his hand. I guessed he'd been in the garden when I arrived, no doubt having a cigar. Family meals did not permit smoking in the conservatory, open door or not.

"Good evening, beautiful family." He made his way around the three of us, issuing us each with a kiss and his characteristic bear-hug, even mum whom he'd spent all day with.

Mum handed him a glass of fizz.

"Not tonight," he said. "Look what I found. Did you bring this, Peter?" He looked at my brother, holding up a bottle of '99 Dom Perignon.

"Not me," my brother said.

"Er, that was me," I said, raising a finger.

What. The. Fuck? my brother mouthed at me.

I shrugged. "Got lucky on a scratch card," I offered.

"Well, that's very generous," said dad. "Glad to see you've inherited my good taste. Now drink up everyone, we're on the good stuff!"

A couple of glasses in, Mum took me to one side.

"I hope I'm not overstepping the mark."

She was about to overstep the mark.

"But my friend Jane has a son. Called Carlton."

He's called what?

"Who is lovely and also happens to be single."

With that name, I was not surprised.

"He happens to work in Cambridge, and I think you'd like him."

I love my dad, but mum and I do not have the same taste in men.

"So here is his number." She offered me a card with a handwritten number on it.

I didn't really have a choice. I took it and slipped it into my back pocket.

"Thanks, mum." I pecked her on the cheek.

"I just hate to think of you alone in that student house. It's nice to have someone to get dressed up for."

I briefly recalled my recent experiences of dressing up (and undressing).

"That is very true, mum. Thank you. I'll call him."

Mum smiled triumphantly before rushing back to the kitchen to deal with a timer that was going off.

Mum always put on a good spread, and the conversation flowed easily over dinner. The usual family jokes made an appearance and several 'do you remember whens?'. It reminded me of the weekend at Fran's. The bits when I wasn't fucking her dad senseless. I smiled.

Then dad tapped his knife to his glass and stood up. I stopped smiling. Such thoughts were now wildly inappropriate.

"A toast," he said.

Any cutlery still in use was lowered and all eyes looked up.

"It's not very often that I have all my family around me, and I hope you will humour me by letting me say a few words."

Peter and I smiled at one another. Dad always got emotional after champagne.

"To my long-suffering wife." He turned to mum. "Thank you for your support and tolerance. Without you, none of this would be here. You are the backbone of this family and my port in a storm. Cheers to you, my darling."

Mum's eyes glistened. "Cheers," we all said, raising our glasses and taking a sip.

Dad turned to my brother. "Peter, my first-born, my boy. Ever focused, a successful businessman, a loving husband, and now a wonderful father. I am so proud of you. Cheers to you."

Peter smiled and we raised our glasses. "Cheers."

Then he turned to me.

"Tilly, my baby girl. Apple of my eye. You have had me in the palm of your hand since the day you were born. It's not easy being the youngest – I should know – but you have forged your own path. Who'd have thought we'd have a lawyer in the family? You make me proud every day. If a little less wealthy." He winked. "Cheers to you."

Then it was my turn to well up.

"Oh, dad," I said. I stood and gave him a hug, wiping my eyes before I sat back down.

Then mum stood up, for once taking the limelight.

"And here's to you, my darling. Who has worked hard every day for me and, when they came along, for the children. We love you. Cheers!"

And that was it. We all stood and with tears rolling, raised our glasses to the ceiling.

"Cheers!"

CHAPTER SIXTEEN

A chink in the curtains let a shard of light fall across the foot of my bed. There was no longer any evidence of my old room being used for laundry. Maybe the ironing had its own room now. I mulled over dad's little speech from last night. How could I now tell him I was thinking of giving up law? And how could I possibly explain it? Then there was the argument with Fran. If I chose escort work would every friendship end once my big secret was out? Part of the joy of this new lifestyle was being able to share the financial benefits. Living a permanent lie just wasn't an option.

Downstairs, I gave mum a kiss while she was busying herself in the kitchen.

"Morning," I said. "Where's dad?"

"Playing golf with Brian." Mum poured me a cup of strong tea from her Denby teapot. "Give me a minute and I'll get you some toast."

The sight of that teapot took me back years and my mind drifted until Mum disturbed my unspecified reverie.

"So," she said as she put the toast in front of me, "you going to call Carlton?"

"Carlton?" Then I remembered. Mum was now a Jewish matchmaker. "Oh, yes. Yeah, why not?"

Did I really want to date a guy from a 1990's American sitcom?

"Promise?" she said.

"Yes." I nodded. "I'll call him."

I actually called Carlton as soon as I got back to my room. I figured the more time I could spend away from the house and Fran, the better. To cut a story short, he answered, agreed to meet, we went for cocktails, then to a jazz club. Though his name was Carlton he liked to be called Jim (who wouldn't?) short for James, his middle name.

After a pleasant evening, we went back to his place (a stylish flat in a converted Victorian semi) and things were going well. He was a good kisser, which is always my 'go/no-go' moment and we got naked in bed, which was also very pleasing. There was some foreplay – not a bad first attempt. And then he mounted me. And the grinding began. At first it was okay. I gave him the benefit of the doubt.

Any minute now we'll change position and things will get interesting, I thought.

But the grinding continued.

I managed to stifle a yawn but when I started to imagine what outfits I might wear to the office, I decided it was time to take matters into my own hands.

"I really love it on top," I whispered in his ear, hoping he'd hear seduction not criticism.

The grinding stopped. "Oh okay."

He seemed wounded.

"Can't have you doing all the work." Just in case, I gave my best ego-soothing smile and then gently manoeuvred him into position. Once he was on his back, I straddled him. Things had dried up somewhat, so I licked my fingers and touched myself.

"Wow," he said, and his cock twitched in appreciation.

Juices flowing, I grabbed him and steered him inside me.

Another *wow*. I had a feeling I was about to blow his mind.

I sank onto him and he gasped.

I rode him and he groaned.

I let his appreciation guide my movements.

"I'm gonna come," he announced as his hands grabbed my thighs.

Grateful for the warning, I concentrated on my own pleasure. My ego dared me to attempt the simultaneous orgasm. It was a feat that ordinarily evaded me, though I'd seen it many times in films so it had to be possible.

I was so close. Then he came and that tipped me over the edge of my own roller coaster. Our groans combined and our bodies slowed to a gradual halt.

"You are amazing," he said.

I groaned, in either agreement or gratitude, he could decide.

Yes, I was. If nothing else, my time as a professional had been a fine education and a fantastic confidence boost.

I must have dozed off because the next thing I knew it was dark and Jim had rolled over, stealing the duvet in the process. I had no intention of staying the night, so I carefully removed myself from the bed, a manoeuvre made easier by the lack of duvet. On tiptoes like a cartoon burglar, I gathered my clothes and left the room to get dressed, then I called a cab and was home and creeping up my own stairs within the hour.

Once home, I lay in my own bed until such time as I could have a shower. It was still really early, and I wasn't sure if Fran was home. I didn't want to disturb her if she was. With only days left at uni, we still had to go in but only to hand in coursework and have final interviews with tutors. I also had a flat to view. Dad was going to help out with the rent initially, so tying up loose ends was my main focus.

Speaking of loose ends… Brenda. Reluctantly, I was starting to think I'd have to call it a day. Of course, I would miss the money, the thrill, the lifestyle, the opportunities – but then I also felt bound by expectation. Working for Brenda was just a little too outside of the box. I knew the life I was choosing was predictable, but on some level it felt right. Didn't everyone make sacrifices? I just couldn't disappoint my family, and I didn't want to live in constant fear of it getting out. Quit while I'm ahead before anyone got hurt, that's what I should do.

I had a good career ahead of me and maybe Jim and I had potential after all. That would please Mum. My time as an escort had been great while it lasted. It had given me so much, and I would always be grateful for that, but it wasn't the life I'd envisaged or that others expected. I'd have to figure out how and when to cut the ties, but right now, I had other stuff to concentrate on. Luckily, Brenda hadn't lined me up with any jobs, so I had some breathing space. Text seemed too impersonal but face to face, Brenda might try to change my mind.

I dozed a little and when I woke again it was just after six, which felt like a more acceptable time to start the day. I got out of the second bed of the night to go for a shower. Fingers crossed there wouldn't be any awkward meetings on the landing with either Fran or any male companion.

Final course work handed in and tutor interviews complete, I turned my attention to packing up the house and literally moving on. I also had a sensible wardrobe to purchase and thanks to Jim, I had a few ideas already.

I had rented my student house fully furnished so I only had my room and a slow cooker to pack, and this all fitted in my car, either in the boot or on the back seat. Amazingly, I'd managed to achieve all of this without bumping into Fran and whilst this was convenient, it was somewhat concerning.

> 'Hi there. Just checking you're okay. Haven't seen you in a while.'

Four hours later she responded.

> 'All good thanks. Got a room in Halls. Let me know when you're done, and I'll come and clear out.'
> 'I'll be out end of the week. Glad you're okay. Take care.'

To which I received no response. However, content that I'd done my bit, I decided to close the book on me and Fran and move on with my new, exciting (fingers crossed) life.

The next day I left the room in the slightly tired, generic state that I'd found it in and moved into the flat that dad was temporarily funding. On the tenth floor of a newish build, the interior was completely white with clean lines and big windows. French doors opened onto a balcony and a great view of the river.

I spent the next two weeks buying soft furnishings and identifying the best local bars and restaurants. I found a sushi restaurant within walking distance and a great coffee shop just around the corner. To top it off, the local pub was renowned for its Sunday lunches and sticky toffee pudding. Jim had popped over a couple of times and things were improving. He had much to learn but was a willing pupil. Unfortunately for mum, I didn't think we'd last much beyond his sexual graduation, but I was enjoying educating him. He would be a real catch by the time I'd finished with him!

The day before I was due to start work, I sat on my balcony with a glass of ice-cold sauvignon blanc. I contemplated the view and imagined my new career. I'd always wanted a career that would impress my dad and outdo my brother and I chose Law after watching *The Good Wife*. I'd then spent years imagining myself in power heels (I'd have to learn to walk in them first) and well-fitting suits and carrying a briefcase that told others I meant business. My reputation would precede me, and I'd be the go-to Brief for the unwinnable case, which of course we would win in style thanks to my tenacity. I leaned back on my chair, closed my eyes and caught a relaxing waft of the potted lavender I'd bought. I just hoped the reality would live up to my expectations.

Day One. I was up early and drinking tea on the balcony, which had quickly become my favourite place in the whole apartment. I'd picked out my outfit the night before and my briefcase was waiting by the front door. I lived close enough to walk to work and I was looking forward to a spot of exercise to start my day, then grabbing a coffee from a cart and sitting on a bench under a tree to change from trainers into heels like they do in Hollywood movies.

Mum called at 7.30 to wish me luck.

"Sorry it's so early, I wanted to catch you before you left."

"That's ok. How are you and dad?"

"Oh, we're fine, he's just left for golf." A pause. I sensed she was building up to something. "You know that whatever you do, we're proud of you, don't you?"

"Of course." *Did I?*

"I know dad went on about you being a lawyer and he boasts about you being at Cambridge, but all we've ever wanted for you and your brother is that you're happy."

"I know, Mum." *Did I?*

She carried on speaking, as if this was something she needed to say and needed to say now. "There will always be people who think they know what's best for you, and maybe they mean well, but the only person who really knows what is best for you, is you. Do you understand?"

Mum sounded determined. Not an attitude I associated with my easy-going, people-pleasing mum. Dad was the advice-giver; mum was there to support whichever hair-brained scheme or idea my brother and I came up with. Ever neutral in family arguments, I wasn't used to her having an opinion, let alone expressing it so vehemently.

"I do understand. Thanks, Mum."

"Anyway," her voice returned to normal and the mum I knew was back in the room. "Have a lovely day. I'll be thinking of you. Bye, darling."

"Bye, Mum." And with that Mum's confessional was over.

I mulled over her advice until I left at eight and then while I walked. I felt strongly that she was speaking from her own experience, but had she missed out on life because of others or was she living her best life despite what they thought? I had a feeling it was the latter but maybe I'd broach the subject next time we were together.

I'd rehearsed the route so I knew I wouldn't get lost, but I wanted to arrive in good time and in good order, not too sweaty. Twenty minutes at a leisurely pace later, plus three to change my shoes (there wasn't a coffee cart and the bench had bird poo on it), I arrived at LFJ Reception ready to start my day in the exciting world of court cases and champagne celebrations.

A young receptionist greeted me and crossed me off a list before presenting me with a security pass that I was to 'take good care of'.

"Somebody will be down to get you in a minute," she informed me, then turned her attention to the next person in the queue.

I took a side step and turned so that I could watch the lift doors. Truth be told, I was expecting a Donna from Suits-type character to waft into the foyer and beckon me forward, so I was a little surprised when a man-child, dressed in a knitted waistcoat that he'd paired with a shirt and bow tie, exited the lift and scoured the area impatiently.

"Tilly? Tilly Young?" he announced in a raised voice.

"Yes, that's me." I walked towards him with my hand raised.

"Cool. Follow me. Mark is a bit highly strung this morning – big court case – and I don't want to piss him off."

"Mark?"

"Yep. Mark Latimer." We entered the lift. "You'll be working with him."

"Do you work with Mark too?" I asked, hoping that the only person I had met in this building wasn't about to abandon me to a stressed-out lawyer on the verge of a big case.

"Yes. Sorry." He extended a soft, manicured hand. "I'm Dan, Mark's PA. For my sins. To be fair, he's not too bad. He's just a little on edge today. It's the last day of this massive case and his nuts are against the wall."

"Oh, okay." What a lovely image.

"Best thing we can do today is keep our heads down and do as we're told. If he says, 'Jump,' just ask, 'How high?'"

"Okay." Today, and maybe tomorrow, I planned to use Dan as a human shield… and do a lot of jumping.

On the fourth floor, the lift doors opened. Around the perimeter of the floorplate were glass-walled offices, each one tastefully furnished and occupied by someone either making notes as they flicked through a pile of papers or speaking on the phone. In the centre was a huddle of desks, each one occupied by a person on a computer, many of whom wore a headset.

"Everyone, this is Tilly," Dan announced.

Heads looked up, smiled, greeted me with a chorus of 'Hi Tilly,' then looked down again.

"Come with me and I'll show you where the coffee machine is." Priorities. Good.

I followed, trying to take everything in whilst ignoring the first day overwhelm that was waiting in the wings. We entered a calm, sunny lounge with chairs, tables, a sofa, and a kitchenette in the corner.

"This is where we come to escape," Dan said. "When all around us are losing their heads." He smiled and gave a flamboyant flourish.

"It's strictly a 'no lawyer zone' so we come here to vent before heading back to our lords and mistresses. Coffee?"

"Yes, please."

Dan handed me a cup of promisingly dark coffee and an open biscuit tin. I took a Hobnob.

"Good choice," he said, taking the same. "So, this morning is *Operation Keep Mark Calm*. Whatever he wants, we get it. We take away all the small shit so that he can focus on the big shit and get ready for this afternoon."

"Okay."

We finished our coffee and Dan washed up the cups.

"Never leave a dirty cup. Mags will do her nut. And you do not want to piss off Mags. She brings in the best homemade cakes."

"Got it," I said, using new words.

We returned to 'the pit' as Dan referred to the collection of PAs and baby lawyers that sat outside the hallowed glass offices. He pointed to my desk, which was opposite his. It was bare except for a desktop computer and a very basic selection of stationery. Some might have argued the stationery selection was more than adequate but without a four-colour clicky pen and a pack of daily mantras, I couldn't agree. I'd just begun to wonder how much personality I could inject into my workspace and still be taken seriously when an attractive blond man with blue eyes and slim hips arrived abruptly in the pit.

"Dan, I've just had Mrs Baxter call me direct. I can't be doing with her today. Call her back and arrange something for Wednesday."

"Of course. Mark, this is Tilly, your new protégé."

"Tilly, morning." He extended his arm and we shook hands. "Bit crazy here today. Let's chat tomorrow."

I nodded. What a pussycat.

Tomorrow came and I was looking forward to my first proper meeting with Mark, to better understand what my time at university, the early mornings and the all-nighters, had been for. I didn't expect huge amounts of responsibility, but I was hoping for the occasional court visit. Maybe I'd get to hand the Barrister some essential paperwork or run in last minute with a crucial witness statement. Maybe I'd watched too many courtroom dramas! Anyway, that morning I dressed like my future self. What is it they say? *Fake it until you make it?* Even I was impressed by the woman in the bathroom mirror, a feeling shared by Dan judging by his welcome when I entered the pit.

"Well, hello Meghan Markle!" He greeted me with open arms and a slight bow.

"Not too much?" I asked.

"Hell, no! You look fine! Your meeting is at 9.30. Can you keep the *va-va-voom* until then?"

"Oh, I think so," I smiled. "Though you may have to make the coffees until I can change into some flats and undo these buttons."

"Deal!"

While I was waiting, I received a text from Jim.

> 'Hope the new job is going well. Would be great to catch up. x'
> 'All good thanks. Will check my diary.'

At 09:29 I stopped pretending to read emails and waited for the numbers to change to 09:30. Mark was engrossed in a ream of paperwork so I knocked on the door. He beckoned me in.

"Morning, Tilly," he said, putting his pen down and tidying the papers he'd been working on. He gestured to a table and chairs on the other side of the room. "Take a seat."

He came over to join me.

"So, welcome to Lloyd, Farmer and Jones. Has Dan been looking after you?"

"Yes, he's been great. Really helped me to settle in."

"Good. I know how daunting it can be during those first few days, and weeks even. So, tell me a bit about yourself."

I gave him a quick synopsis but concentrated on emphasising my eagerness to get started and learn the ropes. If I was going all in, it had to be worth my while. Mark nodded throughout, making the occasional note as I spoke.

"So to begin with, I want you to stick with Dan, understand the work that's done behind the scenes that is integral to your success as a solicitor. I've met many arrogant solicitors who have no idea what they are asking of their staff because they have never been there, so I believe an awareness of what greases the wheels is essential."

I nodded. That seemed fair enough.

"You've got two years here, which might seem like a long time, but you have a lot to learn. You've learnt the law – that's what uni is for, but now it's about work ethic, managing clients, understanding clients, being professional. Applying what you have learnt to the real world. I will push you, you will work late, and you won't always know the answers, but you know what they say… most of our learning is done outside of our comfort zone."

I nodded again. Tell me about it.

"I want you to understand what this job entails, the responsibility, and the personal sacrifices. This is people's lives that we are responsible for and their hard-earned cash that we are taking, and so we owe it to them to perform at our best. No stone unturned. Best effort right until the finish. We may not agree with what we are working on – I've had some shitty cases – but we are professionals and that's what the client sees, not our personal opinions."

"I understand," I said. Sounds intriguing… and somewhat familiar.

"Do you have any questions for me before I release you back to 'the pit'?" he said with a wry smile.

"No, I think I'm good for now." Though I did feel like he'd said a lot without actually telling me anything. Also, it was hard to have questions when I didn't know what I didn't know!

"We'll chat every week and there will be a learning curve. I just want you to spend some time learning what goes on in the background. Okay?"

"Fine by me. Totally understand." I got up to leave.

"Very smart, by the way," Mark said. "Looking the part is key. Our clients have an expectation, and first impressions really do count."

I smiled, feeling really positive about what was to come. I appreciated the need to learn the job from the ground up and I wasn't fazed by the long hours and challenging times ahead. I went off in search of my flat shoes; the discomfort of my heels had been worth it but their job here was done!

Back at my desk, I was crouching over to change my shoes when I noticed Dan escorting a gentleman to Mark's office. I could only see a side profile but there was something familiar about him that I couldn't quite place.

Mark came out of his office to greet him and there was some sort of kerfuffle as they tried to shake hands. In the end, the man offered his left hand and Mark shook that instead. The man entered Mark's office and turned ever so slightly in my direction, at which point I caught sight of his other arm and the cause of all the fuss. A bloody great plaster cast! The penny dropped, or rather it crashed, as I realised why he was familiar. It was bloody George! He who, less than a month ago, had been merrily tossing off behind me while I went down on his wife.

Fuck! I sank even lower and looked around to make sure I hadn't said that aloud. I was still adopting the crouching foetal position when Dan came over.

"Cor, he was fit! Broke his arm cycling in Wales apparently. What an action man!" He looked down at me scrabbling around on the floor. "You okay? You lost something?"

Only my flipping mind!

"Stomach ache."

"Stomach ache?" Dan seemed rightly confused.

"Time of the month. It helps if I scrunch up."

"Oh, I see. Can I get you anything? Paracetamol?"

I shook my head.

"I have been known to buy tampons in an emergency." He spoke the word *tampons* as if they were a class A drug.

"I'll be fine," I said. "I think I might pop out though. Is that client going to be with Mark long? In case he needs me," I added.

"About an hour, I'd say." Then he added, "But don't worry about them. You go, I can handle anything they might need."

"Thank you." I grabbed my bag and made my way to the lift, hunched over with one hand shielding my face and another on my stomach. "I won't be long," I said. I waited for the lift and planned how I might kill the next hour or so.

CHAPTER SEVENTEEN

When I returned to the office ninety minutes later, George had left. Thankfully.

I handed over a cupcake to Dan and said, "I just needed some air."

"I don't need the gory details but thank you." He bit into the buttercream topping and gave me the thumbs up.

The coast now clear, I spent the rest of the day with Dan learning the basics: client bookings, research, printing, filing, shredding… not sure I needed much longer to grasp the 'greasing of the wheels', but if that was the plan, so be it.

When I got home about six I took a glass of wine onto the balcony. I thought back to this morning. Fuck, that was close! What if I'd had to speak to him? What if it happened again and I wasn't able to escape? How embarrassing would that be? The potential for my two lives to cross was real and fucking scary. My palms were sweating and my heart racing at the thought of it.

If I'd been considering my options before, this had put the nail in the coffin. I picked up my phone and typed rapidly.

'Brenda – sorry, can't take any more jobs right now. Got to concentrate on new job. Sorry to let you down. Thank you for everything. Tilly x'

I waited a few minutes for a reply, hoping that it would be something reassuring and understanding.

'Okay.'

That was all I got, leaving me to interpret Brenda's thoughts on the matter.

I felt relieved. Also a little disappointed, maybe… but definitely relieved that I'd reduced the risk of future awkwardness.

My phone beeped and I jumped.

It was Jim.

'Hi there. Do you have plans this w/e? Got tickets for a gig and thought you might like it. Hope so!'

His eagerness was touching but maybe it was time. Our last night together had been most satisfying. It was time to set him free. However, he did deserve more than a text. It was turning out to be an evening of big decisions. He answered after two rings.

"Tilly, hi!"

"Hi, there."

"So, are you up for the gig?"

"Um, I don't think so."

"No problem. Next weekend, perhaps?"

"That's the thing. I had a meeting with my boss today and I think things are going to get pretty full-on. I don't think I'm going to have much time for a relationship."

"I don't mind. I have plenty of hobbies." He had the energy of an excited puppy.

"You're sweet, Jim, but you deserve to be someone's priority."

"Are you dumping me?" Less excited puppy.

"I'm letting you go."

"Oh." Abandoned puppy.

"But I had fun."

"So did I. I'll miss you."

"I'll miss you too." White lie to ease the blow. "But it's for the best."

"If you say so." He sighed. "Bye then."

"Bye, Jim." I hung up before I changed my mind. I'm not made of wood.

I was relieved to have done it. A year ago, it would have been a different story and I understood why mum had wanted me to meet him. He was thoughtful, no obvious ego, caring, attentive… that's a lot of boxes ticked. But I was no longer me of a year ago. I'd moved on, evolved, had experiences, gained independence, grown in confidence. I was also working eight hours a day and earning in a week what I used to easily earn in an evening. Eight hours of photocopying, telephone calls and emails, with a rushed lunch and the occasional birthday doughnut. Not an orgasm or glass of champagne in sight.

I swigged the last of my wine and went inside to prepare dinner that I'd eat in front of the TV before going to bed with a book. I wondered how Fran was getting on.

CHAPTER EIGHTEEN

A month in and I had perfected my phone voice and learnt to make a good coffee in the time it took five pages of printing to finish. Dan had booked a day's holiday to spend time with his mum on her birthday. I was having lunch alone in the lounge. Budgeting measures were in place and lunch was a homemade salad. It reminded me of the time the school dinner ladies had gone on strike and we'd had to take in our own packed lunches and eat in the classrooms. The rest of the pit inhabitants were working through lunch so that they could get away early for Happy Hour. I considered time away from my desk to be more important, so I was going to leave at normal time and catch them up. Whilst I ate, I flicked aimlessly through a magazine that I'd found on the coffee table. It was last month's edition, but I read the horoscope anyway.

'With the arrival of the new moon, you may feel unsettled. Here begins a period of adjustment that brings with it new experiences and opportunities.'

Sufficiently vague and ambiguous as ever. I loved it.

My reverie was shattered by a text alert. Reluctantly, I checked it and was surprised to see that it was Brenda.

'Really need a favour! Can we meet later?'

My stomach flipped. What could it be? Who could it be? Edward? I remembered Fran's comments about how my career would be jeopardised if anyone found out, but the thought of today's mind-numbing to-do list quickly replaced her voice. I messaged back.

'Hi there. Yes, free after 6?' Happy Hour would have to wait until next week.

She texted back immediately.

'Thank you. Meet at The Grange?'
'Of course. See you then.'

The afternoon couldn't pass quickly enough.

"You're in a good mood," commented Alice, one of the PAs.

"Well, it's the weekend!" I smiled and walked over to the printer with a definite spring in my step.

I got to The Grange just after six and Brenda was in her usual chair by the fire. She stood up to greet me.

"Tilly! Wonderful to see you! Thank you for coming." She kissed me on both cheeks.

"Good to see you too." It was good to be back here. I loved how this place made me feel.

"I'd like your help with a new client." I looked up. So, I'd not been brought out of retirement for Edward.

"Hear me out." No doubt Brenda could read the disappointment on my face. She continued her pitch regardless. "His name is Robert Davies, he's thirty-five, and a virgin."

My interest was piqued but I still wasn't sure.

"He feels it's time to lose the big V, so I need someone non-threatening. Someone sensitive."

"I'm really not sure," I said.

"I've met him," Brenda continued. "He's really quite good-looking. Not at all what you'd expect."

I didn't need her reassurance. What he looked like was the least of my worries. "George came into my office."

"Really?" Brenda didn't seem bothered.

"Yes, really. Have you any idea how embarrassing that would have been?"

"I do, as it happens. What do you think would have happened? Did you imagine George enlightening everyone with the tale of how you'd met? Clients want to be discreet too, you know. And besides, Robert lives miles away, you'll never see him again."

I pondered Brenda's rationale. She had a point. Clients wouldn't want it to be common knowledge either. And this job with Robert was going to be a one-off.

"How much?"

"A thousand."

Nice. "Where?"

"The Belfry."

Very nice. A friend's cousin had got married there recently and I remember her telling me how expensive the rooms were.

"When?" Not that I had any plans for the next two years.

"Tomorrow."

Again, I took a moment to consider her request. "Just this once then."

"Oh, Tilly, thank you so much," Brenda gushed. She leaned forward and squeezed my knees. "I owe you!"

I decided to bear that in mind. "No worries," I said, then paused. "Have you heard from Edward?"

"Oh, we catch up every now and then. He asks after you, you know."

"He's a real gentleman."

"Oh, don't think it was the gentleman asking after you."

I smiled and felt myself blush. They had been great evenings.

"Does he still…" How to put it?

"Pay for sex?" I nodded. "Not for a while now. In fact, I think you were his last."

I smiled again.

"So, how's the new job?" Brenda asked.

"I'm sure it's going to be great." I gave a broad smile that failed to reach my eyes.

"That's good to hear," Brenda's smile was equally unconvincing. Sympathetic even. "Anyway, I really need to be somewhere. It's been lovely to see you." A genuine grin now.

I stood up to leave too.

"No, stay. Relax. Finish your coffee. You look frazzled."

I sank back into the leather armchair, absorbing the calm sophistication. A waitress entered the room and asked if I'd like more coffee. I accepted. I was in no rush to leave.

I left just after seven as the evening gym-goers were arriving. Working out on a Friday evening. Now that's commitment! Think I'd be more of a morning person. I picked up a brochure on my way past reception. These twenty(ish)-year-old buttocks would not be here forever!

I checked my text messages and saw two from Alice asking me where I was. Playing catch-up with people with a two-hour head start was not my idea of fun so I made my excuses and went home via M&S, grabbing myself a bottle of wine and a selection of three-for-two Japanese dishes. It was still warm enough to sit on the balcony and when the temperature dropped, I grabbed a blanket, drank my wine, and watched the lights come on across the city.

CHAPTER NINETEEN

Come the next morning the job with Robert was playing on my mind. I sat on the balcony to calm my nerves with a mint tea and a pain au chocolat. I was out of practice and felt like a newbie again. I looked out across the city, trying to take my mind off my worries. When that was unsuccessful, I drained my cup and finished up the last few pastry crumbs.

"What shall I wear?" I pondered aloud as I stood up and went inside to choose a suitable outfit and prepare myself for this evening's nudity.

A taxi picked me up at seven. The Belfry wasn't far from mine but there was no way I could walk that far in the heels I'd chosen. It felt good to revisit this old habit.

The hotel frontage was impressive. Wooden double doors with oversized brass handles towered above a uniformed doorman. He was dressed in a scarlet jacket, black trousers with matching scarlet piping, pristine white gloves, and a top hat, which he raised as I exited the taxi.

"Good evening and welcome to The Belfry."

"Thank you." A wave of contentment washed over me. This is the life.

He pulled open the door (I wondered if he switched arms or whether he had one over-developed bicep) and I entered the luxurious interior, my eyes drawn to a huge chandelier suspended high above the centre of the foyer. I walked carefully across the highly-polished floor in my killer heels, before stepping gratefully onto a huge, Persian-type rug.

"Good evening," I said to the receptionist.

"Good evening," replied Antoine in a faint French accent.

"I am here to meet Robert Davies. Can you tell me which room he is in, please?" I watched as Antoine located the information on the computer in front of him.

He looked up from the computer screen. "Room 501." If his face had an opinion on my being there, I didn't notice.

"Thank you." I turned towards the row of lifts.

On floor five, I stepped out onto a quiet corridor and followed the directions to Robert's room. Outside the door, I took a moment to smooth my skirt and check my make-up and hair. My shoulders went back and I knocked on the door. It opened almost immediately, and I was greeted by an attractive if somewhat startled face. Imagine a cute bunny in the headlights.

"Robert?" I asked. Always pays to double-check before you go down on them.

"Yes." He thrust his arm forward and I shook a slightly clammy hand.

"Hi, I'm Tilly. I believe you're expecting me?"

"Yes. Yes, sorry." He stood to one side, allowing me to enter.

"Can I get you a drink?" Robert asked as soon as I was inside. He appeared to welcome the distraction.

"That would be lovely," I said. Slowly, slowly catchy monkey.

He poured us both a glass of Veuve Clicquot. Probably not his first judging by his rosy cheeks. I took mine and sat on the edge of the bed.

"Come sit down." I placed my hand on the bed beside me to indicate where I wanted him.

Obediently, he came towards me and perched on the bed, his back poker straight.

"Is there anything you'd specifically like to do this evening?" I asked.

"I'm not sure really," he said. "What do you think?"

"Well," I took his glass and placed it with mine on the bedside table. "What I think is that I'm going to start by doing some things that I hope you'll like, and then if you think of anything else, you just tell me. How does that sound?"

"Sounds good," he said with a faint smile and a less startled look in his eyes.

I stood up and turned around to face the door.

"Can you undo my zip, please?" Which he did, fumbling a little.

I turned back to face him and slowly pushed my dress down, stepping out of it when it hit the floor. In my underwear and heels, I stood before him. His eyes were wide and his chin had dropped. I undid the buttons of his shirt. Underneath, his chest was smooth and well-defined. I continued unbuttoning to reveal a toned six-pack.

What a waste. Like an undiscovered paradise.

I undressed him until he stood naked in front of me. He seemed happy with what I'd done so far so I continued by removing my own underwear and heels and placing his hands on my hips. They remained there motionless until I took hold of them again and placed them over my breasts. Once again, his appreciation was evident.

"Do you want to lie down?" I asked.

"Okay," he said.

We lay down next to each other, me on one side, supporting my head with one hand. I travelled my other hand down his chest to his stomach then leaned over and kissed him. His hand moved to the back of my head, and he pulled me gently towards him. I stroked my hand down from his stomach and wrapped my fingers around his cock. I held it firmly and moved my hand up and down. Robert groaned and I felt a familiar sensation of satisfaction and power.

"Do you want to fuck me?" I asked.

"Yes."

I changed position so that I had a knee either side of his hips, then guided him towards me. Slowly, I eased him inside me, then rose up slowly before easing myself back down again.

Robert's eyes were closed, and his hands gripped the duvet beneath us, his hips responding to my rhythm.

"Touch me," I said and gently placed his index and middle fingers. I showed him what I liked, and he continued perfectly. What a good student.

We moved together and I was so close to coming. Was I allowed to come first? Honestly, I had little choice in the matter. I encouraged him to rub me faster and came in a beautiful wave of shooting stars and falling rose petals. Just as mine was subsiding, Robert reached his own climax and came in a rocket launch of pent-up virginity.

I lay down next to him. Cherry popped. My work here is done.

I turned to ask Robert how he was and was greeted by a soft snore.

Bless. I dressed quietly, finished both glasses of champagne, and tiptoed towards the door.

I turned back towards the bed. "Sweet dreams," I whispered before closing the door quietly behind me.

Downstairs in the foyer, Antoine had been replaced by Fionn.

"Goodbye. Thank you," I said as I walked past.

"Goodbye, madam," she replied.

The time on my phone said 21:00. I deserved a late supper. I hailed a taxi and asked to be taken to a little bistro I'd had my eye on.

CHAPTER TWENTY

Monday morning brought me back to reality. There was a pile of shredding that I could have used as a chair.

"It won't take long if we both do it," said Dan. "Then I'll treat you to a coffee and a pastry."

"Reckon we'll deserve it," I said, taking half of the pile. Rock and bloody roll!

The shredding took us forty minutes and then Dan went on a mission to track me down a mille-feuilles.

While I waited, I messaged Brenda.

> 'Saturday evening went well. Thanks for asking me.'

A few minutes later she responded.

> 'No problem. Is that you back on the books then?'

Was it? It was certainly tempting.

> 'Not sure. Maybe...'
>
> 'I'll be in touch then!'

I told myself I was leaving it in the lap of the gods. Who was I to deny my destiny? At that moment, Dan came back holding a paper bag aloft.

"Success!" he shouted triumphantly. "You would not believe how hard these are to find."

"Thank you." I took it from him. There is no dainty way to eat a mille-feuilles, so I made an early apology and dived straight in.

The pastry and coffee were a welcome break from the mundanity of shredding and, quite honestly, the whole array of admin tasks that I was currently employed on. We fully exploited the fact that we were thought to be elsewhere and enjoyed the sanctuary of the coffee room. Dan was telling me about his weekend, but mostly he was filling me in on the gossip from Friday's Happy Hour. By all accounts, there had been a noteworthy amount of illicit snogging and at least one girlfriend who made an unexpected appearance. I reacted as required but all I could think was how insignificant this would seem if he knew what I'd been up to on Friday evening!

"We should get back now," Dan said after twenty minutes.

Reluctantly, I got up and tidied away, making sure to leave no trace of our mini picnic. When we arrived back at the pit, I noticed Mark had someone in his office with him, though they looked a bit young to be a client.

"Has Mark got a new client?" I asked Dan as we sat down.

"No, new trainee. Some girl called Francesca."

I looked up sharply. "Francesca?"

"Yeah, last-minute enrolment. One off the reserve list."

I tried my best to act normal, keeping one eye on Mark's office. After a minute or two they both stood up and shook hands. Her hair was longer but that was definitely 'my' Fran. Could I even call her that now? In the pit of my stomach, I felt a mixture of nostalgia and fear. They left the office and I looked up, desperate to make eye contact and gauge whether I had anything to be afraid of. Mark pointed over to us, obviously identifying 'the pit'. Our eyes met and Fran gave me a little wave, then made a phone gesture with her hand. 'I'll call you,' she mouthed. I nodded and offered a 'thumbs up'.

"Do you know her?" Dan asked.

"Went to uni together." Used to be best mates, though I kept that to myself. I didn't want that conversation.

To my surprise, Fran messaged that afternoon.

> 'Hi there. Can we catch up? Are you free Friday?'

Like nothing had happened! Should I message back? I needed to know if she was a threat.

> 'Yup. 7pm in the Red Lion?'

Somewhere central and with no ties to uni. I wasn't in the mood for nostalgia.

> 'Sounds good. See you there x'

I replied with a thumb . I wasn't ready for kisses.

Friday came and yet again I was making my excuses for not attending the highlight of the working week. I'd not been to a Happy Hour yet and thankfully the desire to have me there was waning. Once again, Dan's puppy dog eyes had failed to change my mind.

"Fine!" he said with an exaggerated flounce. "But don't expect me to share the gossip on Monday."

"I won't," I replied, knowing he wouldn't be able to resist.

Back home I picked an outfit that definitely wasn't student-chic (even though a few favourites still lurked in my wardrobe) but wasn't hooker-tastic either. I settled on trousers and a designer t-shirt that I'd treated myself to after Robert. I'd squeezed in a blow-dry at lunch and was ready to play the part of trainee lawyer, living the dream with a clear plan for the future and absolutely no regrets.

Fran was already at the pub when I arrived and she appeared to be playing the same part. Where were the students of six months ago?

She stood up and intercepted me before I could sit down.

"It is so good to see you!" she said with a broad smile. She opened her arms wide and wrapped them around me. I was caught out by the speed of her charm offensive and my arms remained awkwardly by my side.

"I've ordered wine," she said when we sat down. An unnecessary piece of information seeing as it was in the middle of the table along with two chilled glasses.

"Thank you," I took a gulp, keen to feel the effects.

"I want to apologise." Fran looked down at her glass, ran her finger around the rim then looked back up again. "For the way things ended. I was immature. And judgemental. And selfish. I was scared the plan was changing and I didn't want to do it without you."

I smiled in spite of not particularly wanting to.

"And I was jealous. Of you getting LFJ. But now I'm there too!"

"So how come you're coming to LFJ now?" I found that I cared less for her apologies and explanations, and more for how she'd got a place.

"Turns out my dad went to school with Mark! They got chatting online and when Mark found out I'd been unsuccessful he said he'd pull some strings. Cool, huh?"

"Very cool." I was no stranger to luck and chance, so I had to be happy for her.

"And how are you?" Fran asked. "Are you enjoying it there?"

"I'm getting very good at shredding!" I said with a wry grin. "Though I'm sure it will pick up soon."

We both took a drink. I wasn't ready to dredge up our last night out just yet, so I changed the subject.

"Are you seeing anyone?" I asked.

"No one special. As my dad puts it, I have been sowing my wild oats!"

I remembered the night of our argument and the deep voice I'd heard when she got back.

"Really?"

"Hell, yeah! Making up for lost time." I'd teased her once about how studious she was, and she'd replied by saying that uni was expensive enough without making her dad pay for re-sits. Needless to say, this work ethic hadn't left much time for meaningful liaisons, let alone meaningless ones.

"That's good." Apparently, giving it away for free was perfectly acceptable.

"What about you? You met anyone nice at work?"

I thought of Dan and his liking for knitwear and Abba. "Yeah, but not like that."

"And are you still…?" Apparently, she was happy to revisit our last conversation.

I saved her the discomfort of elaborating. "Nope, not any more."

"Do you miss it?" If only she'd been interested when it mattered. As it turned out, I was glad we were clearing the air – I just wasn't ready to confide in her.

"Course not. It was just a bit of fun anyway."

"Well, I'm proud of you." She reached over and touched my hand.

I smiled again. You know that scene when Jack Nicholson shouts, *'You can't handle the truth!'*? Well, that.

"I did meet someone, and we went out for a bit, but it didn't last." I offered.

I wanted it to feel like old times. I wanted Fran to think it was like old times. We would be working together now, and I needed to have her on side. She had me over a barrel and I doubt she even knew it.

"I only see them once so if the sex is shit, I don't stay for breakfast." Fran countered with a wink.

Oh, the irony! I couldn't help but smile.

"Oh!" She raised her finger to command silence. "I know what I wanted to tell you."

I leaned in.

"Dad's finally seeing someone!"

"Ah, that's lovely!" *Lucky girl!*

"Isn't it? You must have got his juices flowing!" Not the time for a joke about the feeling having been mutual.

We talked about other people on our course and where they'd ended up. Fran was house sharing with one of them but was keen to get her own place once she started earning. She mentioned how Mark had promised her some time in court in the next few weeks. Not before me, I hoped!

At around ten we decided to call it a night. I'd planned to join the gym at The Grange in the morning and it wouldn't do to arrive late or stinking of stale Sauvignon.

"Thank you for coming," Fran said. "I wasn't sure if you would. But it's best to clear the air if we're going to be working together. And besides, there's nothing to fall out about now is there?"

I leaned in and hugged her, as expected. Nothing left to fall out about now that I was leading the life that Fran approved of.

"I'll see you Monday," I said.

"Yes!"

"Yay." I raised clenched fists in celebration before turning and letting them drop.

During the taxi ride home, I stared out of the window, blindly watching the lights of the cars and buildings whizz by. Nostalgia for the times we'd had combined with the residual hurt at how she'd behaved had me confused. Could things ever get back to normal between me and Fran? What even was our normal?

At uni we had been inseparable. We were joined by a common goal and the determination to succeed. But in the outside world, how similar were we? Would we have drifted apart even without the argument, like a holiday romance that fizzles out when returned to normality?

We pulled up in front of my apartment building. It was good to be home.

CHAPTER TWENTY-ONE

Some number-crunching proved that I couldn't actually afford the gym membership at The Grange on my current salary so I threw away my sensible spreadsheet and used my ill-gotten gains to finance it. Decision made, I went all in, ditching my old Rick Astley t-shirt and Ron Hill leggings and splashing out on matching gym kit that was more akin to those fresh-faced humans I'd seen on my last visit. I decided a woman cannot live on photocopying alone and I deserved a treat.

I walked through the foyer of The Grange and felt the familiar sense of contentment at being in such beautiful surroundings. I announced my early arrival at Reception.

"Paulo will be with you in twenty minutes," Jenny informed me. "Would you like to take a seat in The Snug and he will come and find you when it's time?"

"Love to," I said. "Thank you."

A familiar figure sat in the chair by the fireplace.

"Brenda?"

"Tilly! Come and join me." Brenda beckoned me over but remained seated. She looked tired. Not as polished. Less vibrant.

"Are you okay?" I asked.

"Yes, yes, I'm fine. Just busy, and I haven't been sleeping well." She changed the subject. "So how are you? What brings you here?"

"I'm treating myself to a gym membership."

"That is a treat." She nodded in approval.

"I love it here. It makes me feel so sophisticated. It's inspiring." I sighed. "If I'm being totally honest, work isn't great. I needed something to cheer me up."

I was surprised to be opening up to Brenda but now I was doing it, she was the obvious choice. It felt good to get it off my chest.

"Don't tell my mum and dad though… about work, I mean."

"Of course I won't."

"It's not that I don't love the idea of being a lawyer but if I'm honest, a lot of the attraction is proving to my family that I'm as good as my brother."

"Really? But your parents think the world of you."

"I know that now, but he's always been so perfect; good degree, good job, gorgeous wife, cute baby. I picked something that would impress them, something they'd be proud to tell their friends about."

"Oh, Tilly."

"Even the fact that Dad was paying for me to go to uni wound me up. I mean, how bloody ungrateful is that? I told myself he was just indulging me. Indulging me until I realised I was never going to be as good as my brother and gave up."

"But you didn't give up."

"No, turns out I'm actually pretty clever! Also turns out that dad was always proud of me and has always been confident in my ability. It was me that had no confidence in ME!"

"What are you going to do?" Brenda looked genuinely concerned.

"Well, I guess I have to stick it out, at least give it a chance."

"Good idea. It's bound to get better." She changed her expression to mirror my own optimism.

"I bloody hope so." I imagined the pile of shredding/filing/printing that would likely be there on Monday morning. "And now my friend from uni has joined the firm."

"Isn't that a good thing?"

"We've grown apart."

"It happens."

"And she knows. About Edward."

"Oh."

"I didn't want to lie to her any more so I told her. And she flipped."

"People do."

"And now we work together I'm shitting myself that people will find out."

"Would she tell anyone?"

"I don't know," I reconsidered. "Honestly, I doubt it but I can't be totally sure."

"Have you spoken about it since you told her about Edward?"

"Last night. We met for a drink, and I told her it was all over."

"Do you think she believed you?"

"I think so."

"So maybe it's no longer a big deal."

"That's what I'm hoping."

"I think maybe you're overthinking this." Brenda put a hand on my knee.

"Tell me about it!" I smiled at how shrewd Brenda was. "I work with a lovely guy called Dan, and I'm worried that he and Fran will get pally, go to Happy Hour together and she'll have one too many tequilas and blurt it out."

"And if he did know, how do you think he'd react?"

Good question. Disappointment? Admiration? Utter disbelief?

"I have a feeling he'd be more open-minded."

Brenda just nodded. I continued.

"Last night Fran was telling me about her one-night stands and that pissed me off too."

"Pissed you off?"

"Yes! How come she gets to lord it over me when we're basically doing the same thing? She just didn't get it."

"The age-old question," Brenda said wistfully.

"She's such a hypocrite."

"People are."

"And to top it off, I liked working for you."

"And you were very good at it."

"And now I don't know what to do. Especially now that I have nothing to prove."

"Do what makes you happy, Tilly."

"Not that easy though, is it?"

"It never is. But Tilly, you will never please everyone." Exactly what mum had been getting at. "And life is short."

Before I could ask what she meant by that last comment, an accented voice announced Paulo's arrival. "Miss Young?"

"Here!" I raised my hand and stood up.

"Thanks for listening," I said and bent down to kiss Brenda on the cheek.

"I know what you're going through, Tilly," Brenda replied with a hand on my shoulder. "I'm always here."

"Thank you." I turned and followed a toned bottom with a man-bun out of the room.

The gym induction went as expected. There wasn't much that I hadn't used before. As we visited the various machines, Paola put together a training programme, which I promised I would do at least three times a week.

"Consistency is key," Paulo advised as we parted company. "Enjoy your training."

"Thank you." I headed for the aromatherapy sauna before braving an ice-cold shower.

Feeling revitalised and virtuous, I said an enthusiastic goodbye to Jenny on reception, and greeted my fellow gym-goers on my way out. Whatever chaos they had left at home, here they had an aura of calm that I admired. I smiled at the woman I was becoming. You can keep Happy Hour at the local, this was my type of hang-out!

On Monday I wafted into work, still high on purpose and push-ups. It may only have been a spa membership, but it was a step towards the luxurious lifestyle I had tasted briefly with Brenda and was determined to find my way back to. This morning I had my meeting with Mark. I planned to suggest that I had sufficient knowledge of the pit and that I was ready to step up and actually do some solicitor-type stuff. I was eager to use my brain for something other than judging how many pages would block the shredder and I was confident that he would agree.

Fran was already in with him. As they chatted, she did a fist pump and then stood up to leave. As she left his office, she gave me a thumbs up.

"Morning," she mouthed and gave a little wave.

I returned the wave. If Fran was getting good news, then surely, I would too. I gave Mark a few minutes to reorganise himself between meetings before I approached his office.

"Come in," said Mark when I knocked. He moved around his desk and returned to the comfy chair he'd used in his meeting with Fran.

"So how's it going?" he asked once we were both settled.

"Good," I said. Then nervous to get it over with, I launched into my short speech. "I've learnt a great deal in the pit; Dan has been great, and I feel I'm ready to take a step up. To get my teeth into something a bit more challenging."

"I think you're right," said Mark. "I've been thinking the same, but I want to give you the attention you deserve."

I leaned forward. Why the 'but'?

"My concern is that with Francesca's arrival, I won't be able to do that, so I've arranged for you to work with Sasha."

My forehead frowned before I had a chance to feign excitement.

"She's very good. I think you two will work well together. Truth be told, I think Francesca needs more guidance than you and I need to make sure she gets it." He made it sound like he was passing on top secret information, but his performance was wasted. I guessed it was more to do with him and Ryan being old school chums.

I'd met Sasha briefly and she had a great reputation; a bit of a ball-breaker by all accounts, but this sudden move seemed unfair to me. I contemplated making a fuss but what good would that do? Instead, I would seize the chance to learn from a strong female role model.

"Sounds good," I said finally.

Mark then appeared to relax. Had he expected me to kick off? "Great. Dan looks after us both, so you'll have continuity there. You'll do well with Sasha," he repeated.

"I look forward to it." There didn't seem much point hanging around, so I stood to leave. I pushed my arm forward and we shook hands. "Thanks, Mark."

When I got back to my desk, Dan peered over the top of the divider. "Coffee?"

"Yes, please." I could do with a moan.

"Francesca," he called across to a nearby desk. "Fancy a coffee?"

"Ooh, yes please!" she replied.

Guess that moan would have to wait.

And so it was, when we weren't working with either Mark or Sasha, that Fran, Dan, and I became a threesome. And to the outside world, I'm sure we looked like a happy, supportive little trio. If the circumstances had been different, that would have likely been the case, but my feelings for Fran had shifted. She also went to all of the Happy Hours, which I now skipped in favour of a gym session, so her relationship with Dan now included memories that I wasn't privy to along with cosy chats and unexplained giggling.

Working with Sasha was interesting. She specialised in high-profile divorce cases and was utterly ruthless in her support of the aggrieved party, often at the price of compassion.

"I am here to make sure you get what you deserve, so forgive me if I don't dwell on emotions," was often her opening gambit. At which point the snivelling would stop, shoulders would go back, and her client's game face would appear.

"You'll thank me in a year when you're sat on a beach, on a holiday paid for by the generous settlement that I negotiated for you," she said once when her client was slow to adopt the game face.

This laser focus didn't come without its criticism though, and Sasha had quite the reputation within LFJ and beyond.

"Don't you mind that people think you lack empathy?" I once asked her.

"Nope." She continued to highlight her latest case paperwork.

"Aren't you worried it'll put people off?" I pried further.

"Nope." She paused her highlighting and put the pen down. "Tilly, my client does not need a shoulder to cry on. What they need is someone who knows what they're entitled to when they don't and is able to fight for it when they can't. People come to me because of my reputation, not in spite of it. Is it tiring? Yes. Am I always like this? No. Do I cry at airports? Yes. Do I work at an airport? No. Get it?"

"So, it's a front?" I was impressed.

"It's who I am when I'm at work. When I'm not here I laugh, I cry, I eat junk food, and I make excuses as to why I can't get to the gym."

"Do your friends know what you're like here?" I asked.

"Not through experience; I'd never represent a friend, but some of them have heard what I'm like. But they get it. They know the real me. Sometimes you have to be one thing at work and another at home. You'll realise that soon enough." I nodded. I already did. Just a shame that others didn't get it.

It was Friday again. Happy Hour was imminent, and the pit inhabitants were like caged animals, about to be set free.

"Are you sure you won't come?" asked Dan, as he always did.

Friday evening had become gym session number three but maybe, just this once, I could slip it to Saturday? That way I wouldn't drink too much either.

Dan sensed that I was wavering. "Please? I miss our chats. Francesca isn't coming."

"Okay then." Decision made. I was suddenly looking forward to it.

"Fab!" He did a little fist pump. "We leave in twenty minutes."

That left me fifteen minutes to finish my current task and five minutes to refresh my make-up. I caught a glimpse of myself in a mirrored door frame. Maybe I'd make that ten.

Despite my previous misgivings, Happy Hour was fun and at the beginning at least, an opportunity to chat to people I still didn't know that well. My plan to drink responsibly went out of the window after the first end-of-the-week tequila; a pit tradition that I wasn't privy to. The thumping in my head the next morning was testament to the other pit traditions I had enthusiastically participated in.

"Cup of tea?" A male voice from the kitchen.

Dan and I had made a tactical exit after four hours of committed drinking. I'd offered him my sofa when he wouldn't let me travel home on my own.

"Yes, please," I croaked, a consequence of bad karaoke. I grimaced at the memory of my very bad rendition of Berlin's *Take My Breath Away*. A song I always chose, not because it suited my vocal range, but because it reminded me of my first ever slow dance.

"Knock, knock." Dan trilled. He was far too awake.

"Come in." Dan entered with a cup of tea and a pain au chocolat. "Your balcony is to die for!"

"As are you," I said. "Thank you." I sank my teeth into the pastry.

"And what a cute little coffee shop."

I nodded, my mouth still full.

"I'm really quite envious," Dan said. "I'm still living with my mum."

"My dad helps me out." I always felt bad when I admitted that. "But that'll stop soon."

"Wish my dad would help me out," Dan said. "Of course, I'd have to find him first."

"Oh, I'm sorry," I said.

"Don't be. I've never known him so I'm not missing anything." Dan turned to leave. "Oh, yes, nearly forgot. Someone called

Brenda called. Asked you to call back. She wouldn't say why but said to say it's urgent."

I looked up at the sound of Brenda's name and my heart thumped.

"You okay?" asked Dan.

"Yes, fine." Calm down. He doesn't know who she is.

"I'll get off and you can deal with your emergency," Dan said.

"Oh, it'll be nothing. She's a bit of a drama queen." Then, in case Dan thought I meant for him to stay, I added, "But I'd best call her back."

"No probs. Thanks for the sofa. That's the trouble with living out of town; it's a pain to get home after a night out." I got out of bed to see him out.

"Thanks for brekkie," I said.

"My pleasure. See you Monday. I'm glad you came out."

"Me too. Have a good weekend." Dan left and I went to locate my phone.

"Brenda, it's me, Tilly," I said when she answered.

"Tilly, darling. Thank you so much for getting back to me so quickly. I hope I didn't worry you."

"You did a little bit, but never mind." Honestly, I was more concerned that my friend had answered the phone to my pimp. "What's the matter? Are you okay?"

"Me? Yes, I'm fine. I'm just the messenger," she replied. "Edward has asked to see you this evening."

"Edward? Is he okay?"

"I assume so. All he said is that he needed to see you, to speak to you."

"Speak to me?"

"I know. Confused me too, darling."

"And am I…working?" Did I need matching underwear?

"Well, he's paying for your time if that's what you mean so feel free to earn your money!"

Matching underwear.

"What time?"

"Seven."

It was 10:30 now and I still wanted to get to the gym. Plenty of time. "Okay. Tell him I'm free. You sure you don't know what it's about?"

"Not a clue. But I can't wait to find out!"

"You'll be the first to know." Who else would I tell?

"Smashing! Well, I must fly. Speak soon." Brenda hung up, leaving me confused and a little nervous.

My phone beeped and startled me. It was Dan.

> 'Home now. Hope you got emergency sorted. Thanks for the sofa x'
>
> 'All good. Friend wants to see me. Going this evening. Fingers crossed.'

I pressed send quickly before I changed my mind about giving so much away.

CHAPTER TWENTY-TWO

Over dinner I chatted to Edward about work, about my disappointment and frustration at still not having done anything I'd spent the last four years studying for, and that I was now on my second mentor. I told him how I no longer felt the need to impress my parents or compete with my brother but didn't tell him about the signs I kept receiving from the Universe that I should follow my heart and ignore what others thought. I wasn't sure he was ready for that level of 'woo-woo'.

After dinner, we retired to the sitting room. Coffee had been served and the staff had retired for the evening. I perched on the edge of a dark blue, velvet sofa. Edward was standing. Knowing that Edward had something to say, I sat silently, waiting.

"Would you like to sit down?" I asked him.

"I think I'll stand," he replied.

I continued to wait. I hated that the coffee was getting cold, but I was scared that any movement would disturb him as he prepared to speak.

Edward knew my thoughts on lukewarm coffee. "Don't let it get cold."

I poured a cup and took a sip. Good. Still hot.

Then softly, I spoke. "Edward, is there something you would like to talk about?"

"Yes. Yes, of course," he said. "Sorry. I'm nervous."

What on earth was he going to say?

Finally, Edward sat down next to me. He took my hand.

"I received a letter from my solicitor today. My father-in-law has removed the clause from the terms of my inheritance. I'm now free to marry." Would I have to stop seeing him? Don't be so selfish. I put on my game face.

"That's wonderful news. I'm so pleased for you. You'll be venturing onto the dating scene then?"

"I suppose I could. But it's been so long." Edward reached across and took my hand. "And I'm happy the way things are."

"Edward, you have your freedom now. Maybe you should make the most of it." Such a wonderful man should at least give it a go.

"But why?" Seriously? He didn't want it?

"For years you have denied yourself the joy of meeting a soul mate because you could only take things so far. Now you have the freedom to find someone special. Someone to spend the rest of your life with."

"But I already have that." Oh my goodness.

"What do you mean, Edward?" My heart rate had increased. Where exactly was this heading?

"Tilly, I have been living this way for over twenty years. I am reconciled to the fact that I will never have children."

I nodded. Thank goodness. At least it wasn't going in that direction.

"But I also accepted a long time ago, that the opportunity for a soul mate was also behind me."

"Edward," I took his hand. "I know it's daunting, but you deserve this."

"Deserve what? Happiness? What if I am already happy?" He stroked my arm.

Enough beating around the bush. "Edward, do you mean me?"

"Would that be bad?"

"That would depend." I was very fond of this man, but was that enough?

"I'm sorry. I appreciate I am being ambiguous."

"A little." What on earth was he asking me? Should I run now?

"Tilly, I have deep feelings for you. I love being with you."

"And I love my time with you too."

"So, I would like to have an arrangement."

"An arrangement?" I relaxed. For a moment I'd expected him to drop to one knee.

"Yes. Have you ever seen the film *The Blue Bird*?"

I shook my head.

"A girl goes in search of a blue bird. She travels far and wide to find it, only to realise when she gets home that the brown bird she has in a cage is in fact a blue bird."

"Oh." I still wasn't exactly sure where this was leading.

"Tilly, I have the freedom now to search for someone to make me happy, but I have it right here, with you."

"Edward..."

"I am under no illusion that this is a conventional relationship. I also don't expect it to last."

"Edward, please."

"It's okay. I would like to look after you, spend time with you, until such time as you are ready to move on."

"Like a Sugar Daddy?"

"Well, I hate the term, but yes, I suppose so."

I looked at Edward, his heart and soul laid bare. For the first time in years, he had the freedom to choose a future. And he'd chosen to spend it with me.

I took his hands in both of mine. "Edward, I love being with you." Edward smiled and tucked my hair behind my ear. "But, like you say, there is a chance I will move on; meet someone my own age, eventually start a family. And that will hurt both of us. I know you say you don't have time to meet someone, but you do. And you deserve someone who is here for the long haul."

We sat, hands entwined. An amicable stalemate.

"Are you staying?" Edward asked.

"I am," I replied.

Edward stood, held out a hand and pulled me gently to my feet.

Once upstairs, there was no question which room I would enter first. We approached the door to Edward's room.

"After you," he said. He extended his arm forward and stood to one side.

Once inside, we paused. Tonight's conversation, our feelings exposed, hung over us. We undressed, the anticipation as eager as ever. Edward laid me down then knelt between my raised legs and bent down to kiss my mouth. My hands clasped behind his head, pulling him towards me. I felt him touch me, and then he was inside me. He entered me deeply, without hesitation. It was passionate, almost desperate, like we had to finish before we were told to stop. Edward came quickly, leaving nothing behind. I didn't even care that I hadn't.

I lay on my back while Edward basked in his orgasm. I was on the edge of sleep when Edward lifted himself up and kissed me, then travelled downwards. I raised my arms above my head, anticipating his touch. His tongue was firm but soft. Long strokes, followed by faster, shorter flicks until I came, a beautiful release. Edward climbed back up the bed and kissed me. He tasted of pussy. My pussy. I wasn't sure how I felt about that. Not strongly enough to cause a scene. I kissed him deeply.

"I do love being with you, Edward," I said. I rolled onto my side. Edward threw an arm over me, resting a hand on my breast.

"I'm glad," he said.

"Does Brenda know?" I asked.

"Brenda always knows." I smiled. Good old Brenda.

An hour later I was still wide awake, this evening's conversation playing on my mind. Gently, I removed Edward's arm and eased myself from the bed. Edward mumbled but didn't wake. I rummaged in my bag for a pen and notebook.

Couldn't sleep. Decided to go home.
Thank you for a lovely evening.
Speak soon. T x

I left the note where he wouldn't miss it. I didn't want Edward thinking he'd upset me.

Once home, I showered and got into bed. The sheets were fresh, and I fell into a luxurious, dream-free sleep, happy and relaxed in my own space. When I awoke a few hours later, I decided to spend the rest of Sunday in my pyjamas, in quiet contemplation. That lasted for all of twenty minutes.

It was no good. I needed to discuss this with someone. I called Brenda.

"Tilly, darling! How was last night?"

"Interesting. Edward said you know."

"I do. Though I didn't when we last spoke." She added, "I think Edward needed a sounding board."

"I think I need one too. Are you free to meet today?"

"As it happens, I am. Shall we do brunch? The Grange does a marvellous Eggs Benedict."

"Sound amazing. See you there. Thank you."

"Pleasure, darling. See you soon."

Brunch was as good as promised, accompanied by good strong coffee. We avoided the elephant in the room while we ate but as soon as our plates were cleared, Brenda leaned back in her chair and waited.

"So," I began. "As you know, Edward is now free to marry. However, he feels that he has missed his chance to find someone."

Brenda shook her head.

"I know; I feel the same," I said.

"He says he's happy with me and that he would like us to have an arrangement. One that he knows won't last because I will eventually walk away. Brenda, I just don't know if I can do it to him."

"Notwithstanding your burgeoning career in law."

In all the excitement, this had somehow slipped my mind. Great! Something else to consider.

Brenda continued. "This is what I think. He's a grown man, Tilly. He knows what he's getting into. He lost his first wife at a tragically young age. Maybe the thought of you leaving him, however painful you think it might be for him, is less painful than the thought of finding – and then losing – a second wife."

"I hadn't thought of it like that." It made sense and I felt slightly better.

"Tilly, are you happy?" Brenda asked.

"What do you mean?"

"Your life. Does it make you happy?"

"There are bits I don't like; work isn't what I was hoping for, and I'm not earning what I was with you. But that won't be forever."

"That's true. And in a few years, you'll have got to where you could be right now."

I looked up. Depressingly true.

"But do I really want to be supported? I've been supported all my life. I'm trying to be less dependent, not more!"

"So instead, consider the freedom it would give you. The freedom to live your best life, without financial pressure. A chance to leave the career that I'm not sure you really want."

Brenda wasn't pulling any punches.

"Tilly, I've been in this line of work for many years, and I have spent time with many, many men. What I have come to realise is that men need a mate and so, when we are with them, they believe the illusion. They ignore the money that's changed hands, the clock on the wall, the life beyond those four walls, all because, at that moment, they need it to be real. There is something out there that they are escaping, and whatever that might be, it is not there when they are with us. So, if Edward is happy with an illusion, even though he knows it will end, why argue?"

"Men are from Mars; women are from Venus?"

"Exactly."

Out in the car park, Brenda and I said goodbye.

"Not going for a workout?" Brenda asked. I'd arrived with my gym kit and good intentions.

"Not in the mood now. My sofa is calling."

"Boxset?"

"Boxset. Thanks for coming to chat," I said.

"No problem," Brenda replied. "Did it help?"

"It was good to hear your thoughts. I value your experience. Not sure I'm any closer to making a decision, though!"

"You know what I do when I'm out shopping, and I see something I like but I'm not sure whether I should buy it?"

"Buy it anyway and keep the receipt?"

Brenda laughed. "Not quite. No, I imagine how I would feel if I went home without it."

That struck a nerve; I once went home without a pair of corduroy flares that I still regret leaving on the hanger.

"Very wise," I said. "Speak soon." I waved and walked towards my car.

"Take care." Brenda waved back.

At home, I changed into pyjamas, gathered snacks, and made a nest of cushions and blankets. Wine was ruled out for fear that I'd get emotional, or worse still, make a rash decision and drunk dial. Instead, I settled on Dr Pepper and a boxset of *Catching Killers*, which I swapped for *Iron Man* (love Robert D-J) when I realised it was getting dark outside and I was home alone.

I managed to keep myself distracted throughout the film. More accurately, I was high on sugar and unable to sleep. I lay awake imagining how life with Edward might be. I had no doubt that it would have its moments, but I couldn't shake the feeling that I would be moving into a gilded cage having only just flown my last one. I also worried what it would be like when the gilding wore off and I was left in a rusty old prison with the door open but no idea how to survive if I left. Then there was the issue of the day job.

CHAPTER TWENTY-THREE

On Monday morning I headed straight for the lounge to start the day with a strong coffee. Approximately thirty seconds after I got there, I was pounced on by Dan.

"So, spill! Who was the friend? What did they want?"

"Good morning to you too!"

"Sure, good morning. Now tell me!"

I was about to offer a diluted explanation when Fran entered the room.

Great!

"Morning, you two!" she said brightly. "How was Happy Hour? I hear you were there without me."

"It was good," I replied, keen to shut this conversation down. Unfortunately, Dan didn't get the vibe.

"It was a great night and Tilly's place is cool!"

"What? You two?" Fran waggled her finger between the two of us.

"No!" we said together.

"No," repeated Dan in case there was any doubt. "I walked Tilly home then crashed on her sofa.

"Oh. Boring!" Fran seemed disappointed. Surely she knew I wasn't his type.

"Not at all!" said Dan. "Tilly got a phone call on Saturday morning from a mystery woman. Someone called Brenda."

I shot Dan a look that should have read *shut the fuck up* but he misread it and carried on talking.

"Apparently, there was an emergency."

"Sounds interesting." Fran had a look on her face that I couldn't quite translate.

"Not really," I said. I was grateful the conversation was finally back with me. "Just a family friend."

"There you go, Dan," Fran said. "Nothing to get excited about. Sorry."

I smiled and she smiled back.

With the excitement now diffused, I suggested it was time we actually started work. The other two reluctantly agreed and we filed back to our desks like three of the seven dwarves. Dan gave a little 'heigh ho, heigh ho' whistle, which lightened the mood.

Our timing was impeccable; less than a minute after I sat down, Sasha called me into her office. I obeyed without delay, hoping for something worthy of my law degree.

I spent the next two hours helping Sasha get paperwork ready for a meeting later that week. At eleven o'clock she left for a meeting in town.

"This could take some time," she said as she left. "I'll see you tomorrow."

Now at a loose end, I decided to take half a day's leave.

"You jammy bugger," said Dan when I mentioned it at lunch.

"Can I come?" asked Fran.

She'd caught me unawares and rather than respond with a well-prepared (solo) agenda for the afternoon, I gave a startled goldfish impression.

"It's okay, I have work to do anyway," she said.

Inexplicably, I felt bad. I think I was thawing after her earlier efforts to divert the conversation.

"No, you should come. It'll be good to catch up." Part of me actually meant it.

"Fab!" Fran looked as surprised as I felt by my acquiescence. "Afternoon cocktails?"

"Now I'm really jealous," said Dan.

"You had Happy Hour," replied Fran. "Now it's my turn!"

Who knew I was such hot property?

"See you in half an hour?" I said. "I'll email HR and close down my computer."

Fran hopped off her stool. "Me too. See you outside in thirty minutes."

We were both outside in fifteen.

"Anything you need to do?" Fran asked.

"I actually think cocktails are a good idea," I replied. "In fact, follow me!"

I led the way to a place I'd heard some of the girls talking about after they'd been there on a hen do. I'd checked it out online and the reviews were good.

Inside, there was a 1940s vibe. Wooden booths with upholstered bench seats and domed ceilings ran along two sides of the room. Fringed lampshades hung low over the tables and the back wall of each booth was decorated with themed memorabilia.

A waiter in a waistcoat, bowtie, and a floor-length apron approached our table with menus.

"Cosmopolitan?" I looked at Fran.

She nodded.

"Two Cosmopolitans please." The waiter nodded and I took the offered menus for inspiration later.

Our drinks came quickly and we took our first sip.

We sighed in unified appreciation. Just like the old days. We both laughed as we re-lived the memory.

Then Fran spoke.

"That Brenda Dan mentioned… was she anything to do with the escort service?"

"What makes you say that?" Suddenly things weren't so jovial.

"Just the death stare you gave Dan when he mentioned her name. Look, I know I was judgemental – and hypocritical – but you do need to be careful. I stand by the fact that you need to make a choice."

"I know but it's not like that this time."

"It's okay." Fran shrugged. "I understand why you wouldn't want to confide in me after last time."

"No, this really is different. Edward, a client, wants to look after me." I made inverted commas with my fingers when I said *look after me*.

"Like a Sugar Daddy?"

"That's what I called it. I guess so, although he doesn't want to call it that. Long story short, for a long time he wasn't allowed to marry because of a clause in his wife's will. Now it's been removed, he's decided he still doesn't want to marry but would like to take care of me."

"And how do you feel about that?"

"Like I'm taking a step backwards." Finally, I'd said it out loud.

"That's honestly what I'm thinking too."

"Really?" Thank goodness! "I feel so ungrateful for not snapping his hand off."

"Look, when I met you, you had no confidence, illustrated by the fact that you spent far too long going out with that creature, Jed. Then you started working with Brenda. You had money, you were independent, your confidence grew. Basically, you shone! I didn't really notice at the time but now I look back and it really was a transformation. Not to mention the miracle you worked on my dad!" I felt myself blush. "So, should you say yes to being looked after? No, I'd say. You don't need it. You've come too far."

I had tears in my eyes when Fran finished. Our short-lived, intense friendship had meant something after all. It had been real. Fran had really seen me.

"Thank you." I reached across the table and held her hand. "I've needed to hear that. It's what I think too."

"And what about the escort work? Is that finished now?"

"I did one job. But it was an emergency, a one-off."

Fran gave me a look. "I just don't want LFJ to find out before you're ready to make a decision," she explained. "Do you know what you're going to do long-term?"

I caught the waiter's eye and gave him the international sign for 'two more of those please'.

"I know what I want to do."

"Work with Brenda?"

I nodded.

"So why don't you?"

The drinks arrived and I waited for them to be placed on the table and the empties cleared.

"No reason. Other than social norms, parental acceptance, the borderline legality of it all."

"That's quite a list. What is it you like about it?"

"The money. The life I can afford with that money. The confidence it gives me. The sense of accomplishment when I give my client the experience they hoped for. The working hours. The freedom. But it's all overshadowed by the negatives."

"So why tell people? You don't need to tell everyone everything. Say you're an entrepreneur; make something up."

"Maybe."

"And I'm sure Brenda can help you stay on the right side of the law."

"True." I nodded. I had no doubt Brenda would be there to advise.

"So, let's toast to the future. Whatever that might be." Fran smiled and her enthusiasm was contagious.

We chinked glasses.

"Can I say," I continued tentatively, "without offending you, that you've changed your tune?"

"You can."

"Any particular reason?"

"My mum died." Fran bit her lip and her eyes moistened.

"Oh my god!" Instinctively, my hand lifted to my open mouth. "I'm so sorry!"

"Thank you." Fran wiped tears from her eyes. "Honestly, I don't think it's sunk in yet."

"How? What happened?" I was too shocked to consider that the framing of this question might have been insensitive.

"Cancer. Really fucking quick cancer."

"Oh Fran, I'm so sorry." Briefly, I imagined myself in the same position. The feeling was unbearable. "How's your dad?"

"Okay, considering. Think that's another reason why he's stopped dithering and started dating again. Life's too short."

I remained silent and let Fran speak.

"So, in answer to your question, I realised that we're not here for long and that while we are here, we should do stuff that makes us happy."

"Cheers to that!" We chinked again.

Two Sexes on the Beach, two Mojitos, and two Tequila Sunrises later, we decided to move on. We thanked Jules, the waiter whose name had been requested after round three, and walked carefully to the door, trying our hardest to act like young women who hadn't been drinking all afternoon.

"I think I should go home," I said.

"Me too," Fran replied.

"Want to stay at mine?"

"Well, you do have an amazing balcony."

"I do."

"Yes, please."

As it happened, we slept in my king size and Fran insisted I tell her about my 'jobs'.

"You went down on a girl?"

"How old was the virgin?"

Bless her. Not long ago I'd have been asking the same questions.

"What time is it?" asked Fran as the morning sun streaked across the bed.

"Seven," I replied.

"Thank fuck," she said. "I hope you have a good shower."

"The best," I replied, lifting a pounding head from the pillow. "You shower and I'll do coffee."

I was more like my mother than I realised.

Fran appeared in the lounge. I handed her a cup of coffee and a croissant.

"Amazing bakery downstairs," I said in response to her *what the fuck is this kind of service?* face.

Fran made her way to the balcony. "Well, this is as lovely as Dan said it was," she shouted over her shoulder as she stepped outside.

"Sure is," I called back before taking my turn in the shower.

It had been good to spend time with Fran. I'd missed her friendship, and I was glad we'd finally had a grown-up discussion about things. The fact that she knew my deepest, darkest secret was a relief and a worry in equal measure. I liked having her support, but it also made me feel incredibly vulnerable. But I knew why. It was all about LFJ. I was paranoid that they would find out and I'd be asked to leave, in disgrace. I needed to make a decision. But first I had to get through today with a hangover that was getting bigger by the minute. I put on some make-up in the hope it would hide the evidence of school-night drinking, then poured a coffee and joined Fran on the balcony.

"I am very lucky," I said, a belated response to Fran's earlier comment.

"I think you had a lucky start, but you've done the rest yourself."

We sat in amicable pastry-eating silence.

"I am sorry I was such a judgemental cow," Fran continued. "What you do… it's not for me, but I do envy your courage."

"In the beginning, I did it for the money. I needed money quickly and freaked out. It was less about courage and more about necessity."

"But you did it again?"

"I enjoyed it." I checked Fran for a reaction. Her face remained passive. "If I didn't, I'm not sure the money would matter that much."

Seemingly satisfied, Fran popped the last of the croissant into her mouth. "Shall we go?"

I checked the time and sighed. "I guess so."

As we were leaving the flat, I touched Fran on the shoulder. "You won't mention this to anyone, will you?"

"Of course not."

"Not even Dan."

"Not even Dan."

"Thank you," I said. "Roll on home time."

"Hear, hear," Fran replied. "I have paracetamol."

"Already taken some."

We laughed. Life on the edge!

CHAPTER TWENTY-FOUR

That weekend I had important things to do. It was two weeks since I had seen Edward, and he deserved an answer. I also had a letter to write, and I wanted to see Brenda. I messaged Brenda and asked if she could arrange for me to see Edward on Saturday.

'Do you have an answer for him?'

'I do. And are you free on Sunday for a coffee?'

'I am. 11am suit?'

'It does. See you there.'

She messaged back twenty minutes later to tell me that Edward's car would be at mine at six on Saturday.

I arrived at Edward's and he was outside to meet me. He opened the car door and offered me a hand.

"Forgive my eagerness," he said. "I've missed you."

"I'm here now." I kissed him on the cheek.

"You are." He kept hold of my hand and led me inside.

In the sitting room, he poured champagne and handed me a glass. "I am hoping you come here tonight with a decision."

I nodded.

"Do you mind telling me now? Whether it's yes or no. I hate to put you under pressure, but I can't relax until I know."

"Okay." I took a sip of the champagne and I reviewed my decision for a split second. This decadence would be my life, this attention and admiration an everyday occurrence. It would undoubtedly be wonderful. Or would it? Would I feel trapped? However long the leash, would I still feel its pull? Would I be free to live the life of a twenty-something-year-old or would I feel guilty when I wasn't with him? But it was too late for these thoughts now. I'd already approached it from every angle.

"Sit down," I said. He sat quickly and took my hand.

"Before you start," he said. "I want you to know that there is no wrong answer. You are free to choose however you wish."

That did make things easier.

"Edward, I want you to know that I love the time I spend with you. This lifestyle is truly wonderful. The nights we spend together, the lovemaking (I wanted to say sex but felt that he was more of a lovemaker) is amazing. And all of that, I never want to end."

I took a sip of champagne. *Don't start with a 'but'.*

"My whole life, I have received financial support. I needed it but I was also conscious of how reliant I was on my father's money." Edward nodded, encouraging me to continue. "It's really only now that I am beginning to stand on my own two feet. I am making my own money, my own decisions, decisions that now have consequences."

I was talking quickly now, the passion rising within me. Edward's expression remained neutral as he calmly allowed me to speak. "For the first time, I feel like I'm not playing at life. It's scary but it's what I want; to prove to myself that I can do it."

I took a deep breath. Edward did the same, knowing his answer was imminent. "So, I'm going to decline your offer." Again, I looked at Edward, checking his body language. He smiled weakly. I made an attempt to soften the blow. "I love what we have now and I want this arrangement to continue. But any more would feel restrictive. And I know you wouldn't control me. I know that I would be free to come and go," I added quickly, fearing Edward would try to disagree. "But I need to spread my wings, to explore my potential. Alone. So, if you are willing, I would like things to stay as they are."

I sat still and waited for Edward's reaction.

Edward fidgeted with his hands before responding. "I knew I was asking a lot of a woman of your age. You have your life ahead of you, but I had to ask. Maybe with the changing of the will, the freedom went to my head, and I panicked. If you say that things won't change then I am content. I just couldn't bear to lose you."

"You won't."

Edward sat back down and kissed me. If there was ever a relieved kiss, this was it. I moved to sit across him. He fumbled with his belt and I unzipped his trousers. We shuffled and manoeuvred clothing. My dress was pulled to my waist, my lace panties to one side, revealing a neat Brazilian that I'd tried for the first time yesterday.

Up until now, I hadn't been sure whether I would repeat the experience owing to the pain required to achieve it. However, looking down I was changing my mind. Edward followed my gaze and seemed equally taken with the look. However, this was not to be a 'stark naked on the polar bear rug' type of moment and that was as far as the undressing went.

As we kissed, he entered me. After two weeks apart, his cock felt especially good. Edward groaned as he went deeper, and I guessed he felt the same. Our bodies moved confidently together, two separate dances moving as one. The location and the sheer audacity of this sex (no lovemaking here) must have added an extra frisson because I climaxed quickly and surprisingly loudly.

My back arched as I came and Edward's hands gripped my waist. As I was finishing, Edward reached his own climax. I was tight from my own orgasm and his hands pushed me down hard as he shuddered and groaned.

We sat entwined for a moment.

"I need a shower," I said. Eau de post-coital was never going to catch on.

"I'll get some food together. What would you like?"

"I'd really love a pizza."

"Okay," he said. "Are you happy with takeaway? It's not something we normally have in."

"That'll be fine."

"But I have to warn you," he said. "I have pineapple on mine."

I laughed. "I forgive you." After all, it was possibly his only fault.

We both showered and arrived back downstairs in our robes. We ate the pizzas on the sitting-room carpet, with glasses of champagne. Slutty decadence.

I decided not to stay the night and we made love again before I left. This time it was naked, and on a rug, though still no polar bear.

"See you soon?" he asked as I left.

"Of course. Let's get something in the diary." I kissed him on the cheek.

In the back of the car, I laid my head back, closed my eyes, and searched for any hint that I had been wrong to decline Edward's offer. I was relieved to feel no regret, just a lightness from having had the conversation I'd been dreading.

CHAPTER TWENTY-FIVE

Sunday. My meeting with Brenda. I arrived in good time, gave Katy on Reception a wave, and made my way directly to the Snug.

As ever, Brenda sat in her corner seat. I wondered what she'd do if someone else sat in it. Again, I was struck by her appearance. Her make-up and hair were on point, but she looked different somehow. She looked up so I broke my stare and greeted her. She didn't stand so I bent to hug her.

Service was as slick as ever, and coffee arrived not long after me.

"So, Edward?" Brenda gave a cheeky smile.

"I turned him down."

"I knew it," Brenda said. "How did he take it."

"Surprisingly well," I replied, remembering the two times he'd reacted last night.

"But you'll continue to see him?" she asked.

"Of course!"

"And LFJ? Has it got any better?"

"Actually, no but I'll think of something." I was keen not to dwell on that particular conundrum. "But what about you? There's something going on, isn't there?"

"I've been poorly," she replied.

"Nothing too serious, I hope."

"Oh, a touch of breast cancer," Brenda said with a wave of her hand.

"Oh, Brenda!"

"Don't worry, darling. They caught it super early, and I'll be fine." She took a sip of coffee. "But it has made me realise how fragile everything is. So, for my sins, I plan to spend more time with Brian. I've invested wisely over the years, so I can afford to slow down.

"I hate to ask, but what about the business?"

"I'll think of something," she replied ironically. Then, more seriously, she said, "I have a couple of people in mind to take the reins. If this has taught me anything, it's that life is short. I'm not going to waste time worrying."

"Life is short," I repeated. "That's what Fran said to me."

"Fran? So, you're friends again?"

"I think we might be." I smiled at the thought.

"That's good. We need people."

We finished our coffee in silence then Brenda made a move to stand.

"Time I left. Feeling weary." She did look tired.

"I'll walk you out."

We walked arm in arm to the car park and I dropped her off at her car. Before she closed the door, she took my wrist.

"You'll be okay, you know. Just don't be afraid to make bold decisions. The Universe rewards those that take chances."

"Thank you. Take care." I blew her a kiss and pushed her door shut.

This time I did go back to the gym for a workout. Half an hour on the treadmill would be good thinking time.

The next week went by without incident until I was woken up by butterflies on Friday morning. A boisterous flight of them in my stomach. Ever since school, this feeling indicated some sort of challenge in the day ahead. I looked over at my bedside table and the letter that I'd written yesterday. I had re-read it twice before attempting to sleep. Then I'd dreamt of my teeth falling out and finding myself naked in a meeting. Honestly, it was a relief to wake up. Ordinarily, I'd have given myself an extra ten minutes under the duvet, but I couldn't relax with that feeling in my stomach, so I got out of bed straight away.

While the kettle boiled, I busied myself with a few stretches in front of the French doors. It was comforting to see that the city remained the same despite the changes I had planned. I drank tea and ate toast whilst jigging to the songs on the radio. Sitting still would just encourage the butterflies. I continued the distraction technique in the shower, where I added bad singing, and I could feel my mood lifting. Maybe I should start every day like this! I grabbed my letter and cha-cha-ed out of the flat. Okay, Universe, let's do this!

I walked into work and up to reception with the bank of pigeonholes behind. I put my hand in my bag to hand over my letter to Raquel, today's receptionist. Best get this over and done with. At that moment Dan arrived behind me.

"Morning, gorgeous!"

"Morning. You're in a good mood!"

"I had a wonderful evening," he said with a wink.

"Oh, really?" I removed my hand from my bag. *I'll do it later; I promise* I said to myself when I heard the mind monkeys doubting my commitment.

Dan and I walked together towards the pit. I'd no sooner arrived than Sasha poked her head out from her office.

"Tilly, can I have a word please?"

"I'll hear all about your shenanigans later," I said to Dan as I went off to see what Sasha wanted. Again, the mind monkeys got involved, asking what I'd done wrong, what I'd forgotten. Maybe it was that afternoon off work. "Oh, shut up," I said under my breath in response to their mithering.

"Morning, Sasha," I said with a big smile.

"Morning, Tilly. Take a seat please." The smile was not returned.

Oh, bollocks.

"Last week when I had a meeting in town." Shit, it *was* about the afternoon off! I opened my mouth to explain, apologise, beg. Sasha continued. "I found out I'm pregnant." I opened my mouth again, this time in amazement. Sasha caught my expression. "Trust me, I felt the same. Six months gone and I had no idea!"

I didn't know whether this was good or bad news for Sasha, but I did know it was bad news for me. As far as I'm aware, even machines like Sasha do not give birth surrounded by case paperwork and then carry on as if nothing has happened.

"So, what we need to discuss, Tilly, is what happens with you whilst I am away on maternity leave." She'd evidently read my mind, which was better than me raising the subject. That felt trivial in the face of Sasha's life-changing event.

"Obviously, Mark is mentoring Fran so we have decided that Steve would be the next best fit."

Steve was about fifty and was known mainly for his sweaty armpits.

"Steve?"

"Yes. He's actually a good operator. You'll learn a lot." She used the same tone that Mark had used when he'd palmed me off on Sasha.

"Okay," I said. Though obviously it wasn't.

"I'm aware your time here hasn't been as smooth as you would have liked."

"No problem." I felt deflated, let down, but what else was there to say? "Congratulations, by the way."

"Oh, thank you. It's not sunk in yet." Instinctively, Sasha touched her belly.

"Is there anything else?" I asked.

"Actually, there is. I wasn't going to mention this, but it looks like you need something to look forward to." That sounded promising. I decided to listen. "We are expecting a high-profile case in a month or two. I expect there will be media attention and it'll be a huge professional boost for whomever it's awarded to. Whoever assists on it is sure to get a leg-up too; it'll be a fantastic experience. I'm really quite envious, but I can't have everything."

She smiled and for the second time placed her palm protectively across her stomach. "Anyway, I'd like to put your name forward to assist. You're definitely good enough, but I think after everything, you deserve it."

"So I wouldn't work with Steve then?" I asked.

"Not if you were successful. And as the most senior of your peers, I'm confident of your chances."

"Sounds good. Thank you."

"Just keep it under your hat for now."

"Will do."

Meeting over, I went back to my desk, took my letter out of my bag and placed it at the back of my top drawer. There just in case. I'd give Sasha a chance to fight my corner. I'd seen how persuasive she could be.

"Who's for dinner later?" I said to Fran and Dan. "I believe Dan has some news!"

We sat in the local Wetherspoons, waiting for our orders to arrive. "Well?" Dan was being surprisingly unforthcoming.

"Me? Oh, I hooked up with Lewis." Lewis was his ex whom he had vowed never to touch again even with a rusty barge pole.

"Oh, Dan!" Fran and I chorused.

Dan waved away our remonstrations. "Whatever! Anyway, what about you?" He pointed at me, and Fran switched her gaze in the direction of his finger.

"Me?" Which part of my life did he need explaining?

"The meeting with Sasha. What was that about?"

"Sasha is pregnant and I've been moved across to Steve."

Fran cringed.

"I know. But he's really experienced. I'll learn a lot."

"If you say so." She sounded about as convinced as I felt. Shame I'd been sworn to secrecy about the little sweetener I'd been offered.

At that moment, I was rescued by my phone ringing. It was Brenda. I excused myself and went outside to take the call.

"Hi, there. You okay?" I was forever paranoid now that she would take a turn for the worse.

"Yes, darling, all good. I just wanted to let you know that I'm meeting with a potential replacement tomorrow."

"Replacement?" I was being slow.

"For me. To take over the business. An old friend who has her own agency and is looking to expand."

"Oh, I see." My reaction to this news shocked me. "Thanks for letting me know."

"No problem. I figured you deserved a heads-up."

"Thanks. Listen, I've got to go. Speak soon?"

"Yes, darling. I'll let you know how my meeting goes. Bye then."

"Bye."

I hung up. My heart was thumping as I went back into the pub.

"Can I talk to you?" I grabbed Fran's arm.

"I guess so," she replied as I dragged her to the toilets.

I checked that we were alone. "What's wrong?" she asked.

"I don't know what to do."

"Okay. Any more information?"

"Brenda is retiring and she's found someone to take over the business."

"Why is that bad?"

"Because I think I want it."

"What? Seriously?"

"I think so."

"Okay. So what's stopping you?"

I paused. "There's a high-profile case coming to LFJ and Sasha's going to put my name forward to assist on it. It would be great for my career, really give me a head start."

"So now you want to stick with law?"

"I don't know. If I get this case, then maybe."

"And are you likely to get it? Is there much competition?"

"Dunno. Sasha reckons I stand a good chance."

"So what's the problem?"

"What if I don't get the case but by then Brenda has retired and I've missed the boat there as well?"

"That is a risk."

"Exactly."

Fran took a deep breath. "Tilly, my mum died aged forty-two of a disease she only knew she had for three weeks. I used to hate her for leaving my dad and running away to Scotland but now I'm glad she got away and at least started to live the life of her dreams." She paused but wasn't finished. "Have you ever heard the saying, 'Those that mind don't matter, and those that matter don't mind'?" I shook my head. "Well, that's kind of my mantra now."

"Would you mind if I did it?"

She smiled and reached for my hand. "I am touched that I matter again and for the record, no, I wouldn't give a shit!"

"But ditching a respected career in law to run an escort agency, wouldn't that be bad?"

"According to whom? You have to please yourself in this world, Tilly."

My mum's words on the phone came back to me. "I suppose."

"I can't make the decision for you."

"I know."

"Imagine yourself in a year's time. In one scenario you were chosen to assist on the case and your career has really taken off as a result. In the other you've taken over from Brenda and you're living that lifestyle. Which one is more exciting? Which one gets the juices flowing?"

Unfortunate turn of phrase. I smiled.

Fran giggled. "You know what I mean."

I sat for a few seconds, playing the two scenarios in my mind. I'd lived the 'Brenda lifestyle' and loved it. Then again, a successful career in law would be exciting too. Also, long hours and high stress, but satisfying in its own way.

"There's so much to consider," I said aloud.

"Like what?" Fran would make a great therapist.

"Do you remember what I was like before? How I thought I needed a boyfriend?"

Fran nodded. "That Jed was a right minger."

"Don't remind me."

"But you're not like that now. I mean, you dumped Jim and he had potential!"

"And there's a reason I'm not like that now. Working for Brenda. Yes, I was helping the clients, but it was helping me too."

"Sounds to me like you know the answer," said Fran. "So, what are you going to do about it? Hurry up, our wine will be getting warm!"

What was I going to do about it? Time was ticking and only I could stop the clock. I pulled my phone from my pocket and typed a message before I had a chance to change my mind.

I simply wrote:

'Let me take over.'

I showed Fran and she raised two sets of crossed fingers.

The reply was on its way.

'I thought you'd never ask!'

"Come on," I said to Fran. "I'm buying champagne."

CHAPTER TWENTY-SIX

I rolled over and was greeted by warm beer breath. I turned to the other side and was met by a set of painted toenails. I lifted my head, which weighed at least two stone, and looked around. All three of us were in our underwear, although Dan was not as covered up as I would like. I admired Fran's matching lingerie – shame she had wasted it on us. It occurred to me that Fran might be one of those girls who shaves and wears nice knickers even when she's single, something that even now, I only aspired to for professional reasons.

I weighed up my various escape routes and decided that my arse in Fran's face was preferable to being caught with my boobs in Dan's. I moved like a sloth and was as quiet as a parent swapping teeth for money. No sooner had I left the bed than Fran and Dan both rolled over and absorbed the space. I grabbed my robe and crept out of the bedroom.

I needed tea. I gathered the constituent parts of the life-saving beverage and opened the French doors while the kettle boiled. The fresh morning air was a pleasant change from the scent of stale, sweaty bodies and I inhaled deeply. I sniffed my armpits and exhaled into cupped hands. Ripe! A shower would be next on my to-do list.

The only good thing about a hangover is how good it makes a cup of tea taste. The hot liquid cut through the dead-badger lining of my mouth and revived me as well as any good first-aider. However, I knew this chipper state wouldn't last long so I made my way to the shower without delay, and emerged minutes later feeling refreshed and smelling of lemongrass. Dan had moved from my bed and had taken up the same position on my sofa. Thankfully, he was now wearing trousers.

"Tea?" I asked, to which he grunted.

"Coming right up."

At that moment a less grunty Fran entered the room. Apparently keen to give her underwear the audience it deserved, she hadn't bothered to apply more clothing.

"Morning," she said. "That was quite some night."

"Was it?" I asked. "Did I…?"

"Sing your usual karaoke? 'Fraid so. Though I think you're getting better."

"No, she isn't." Dan had found his words.

I brought over two cups of my magic tea. "Shall I make toast?"

"With Marmite please."

"Jam for me."

We sat for a while with nowhere to be, piecing together the events of the previous evening. Thankfully, no-one had shamed themselves or snogged anyone, most people had danced to *The Birdie Song* when I'd requested it, and we'd all acted like responsible adults in the taxi. Whether we'd stripped as part of a game or out of necessity was still a mystery, but by then we were back at the flat with no other witnesses, so we didn't care.

Fran got up. "Well, I could stay here all day, but I have shopping to do. The joys of living alone."

"And I promised my mum I'd mow the lawn. The joys of living at home." Dan got up too.

I offered the use of the shower but they both declined. "Best not. Time's ticking." was the paraphrased reply from the pair of them.

My phone beeped.

> 'See you at 3?'
> 'See you then'

OMG! Shit just got real!

Brenda and I met in one of the private rooms. I wasn't sure what level of detail we'd have to go into but better safe than sorry.

This time, Brenda stood to greet me. She looked well, and I told her so.

"Cabbage water and turmeric," she divulged.

"Sounds lovely."

"It isn't. But it promises miracles."

I nodded. I had a feeling her improved appearance had more to do with traditional medicine but who was I to argue?

We sat.

"First of all, thank you. Though I didn't let on, I did have my concerns about the future of the business, and as you can imagine, I do not need to be worrying at the moment."

I nodded in agreement.

"Before my colleague came forward, I was thinking I'd have to hand it over to Michelle. Not a prospect I was looking forward to."

From what Brenda had said in passing, Michelle (not her real name) was in her forties and specialised in married men on business trips.

"Don't get me wrong, Michelle is fantastic in her niche but she's not a businesswoman. As for you, my darling…" She smiled broadly. "I am so excited by what you will bring to the party."

"Me too. Though I'm not sure what that will be just yet!"

"Don't worry about that. In the beginning, I think, just keep things ticking over. Learn the ropes before you make any changes, if indeed you feel that's necessary."

I certainly wouldn't be making changes just for change's sake.

"So, how do I pay you for the business?" I got straight down to the nitty-gritty.

"Good question. I was thinking a monthly commission. Unless you would prefer to buy me out?"

I had savings but not the amount I assumed would be needed for that. "I think a monthly commission would work best. Would you still be on hand to advise? At least while I'm finding my feet?"

"Of course, darling. Listen, I'll get my solicitor to draw up a simple contract. That way we both know where we stand."

"Sounds good. Thank you," I said.

"How do you feel about leaving LFJ?" Brenda asked.

"Liberated!" I said with a smile.

"And what will you tell your parents?"

"I'll tell them a business opportunity in hospitality came my way. Dad will appreciate the entrepreneurship." After the shock had subsided anyway.

We chatted for a bit longer while we finished our coffees.

"I'll be in touch when I have the contract," said Brenda.

"Sure," I replied. "I'm off for a swim. Do you want me to walk you to your car first?"

"Thank you. No, I'll be fine." Brenda kissed me goodbye. "See you soon." She gave a little wave and sashayed out the room. Maybe I should try cabbage water!

CHAPTER TWENTY-SEVEN

As soon as I arrived at LFJ on Monday morning, I headed for my desk, grabbed the letter from the drawer and marched it straight over to reception. I handed it over. Quick and without unnecessary thought, like pulling off a wax strip.

"Morning Raquel, this is for HR." She placed it in the pigeonhole with a nonchalance that jarred against my own adrenalin, which dissipated once my resignation was literally and figuratively out of my hands.

"What was that?" Dan asked when I got back to my desk. He seriously never missed a thing.

I took a deep breath. "Come with me." I led him to the coffee room. With the door shut, I prepared myself to say it out loud for the first time.

Here goes. "I'm leaving." It felt okay. Good even. I smiled.

"What? Not the Steve thing? You can't leave because of that!"

"It's not that. An opportunity has presented itself and I need to go for it now or I'll miss the boat."

Just then Fran entered the room. "I thought I'd find you both here! Where was my invite?"

"She's leaving," Dan blurted out.

Fran did the goldfish and shrugged, looking to me for guidance on how she should react.

"She already knows." Fran's facial expression returned to normal.

"What?" Dan looked downcast.

"She was there when I got the call." A little white lie to soothe his hurt feelings.

"Okay. I'll let you off." In many ways, Dan was a typical bloke. Not holding a grudge was one of them. "I'll miss you."

"And I'll miss you too," I said.

With no time for further details, we group hugged and reluctantly went back to work. Back at my desk, a tsunami of lethargy washed over me so I made a spontaneous decision to book annual leave. I had three weeks owing to me and my notice period was four. If I saw out the rest of this week I could slip away with minimal fuss and avoid the inevitable invite to my final three Happy Hours.

In the days that remained, I would clear my desk. A few bits every day so as not to draw attention to my departure. Fran had always admired my fluffy cushion and Dan was a sucker for a pot plant so I could give away the stuff that wouldn't fit in my bag.

Sasha requested another meeting on Wednesday, once HR had had a chance to process my resignation. I made it clear that my decision was not a result of our meeting on Monday and she asked why I hadn't mentioned sooner that I wasn't happy. I wondered that too. Maybe I hadn't wanted things to be better.

"It's certainly a brave decision, especially after all those years at uni."

I nodded.

"I admire you," she said. That was unexpected. "Best of luck."

"Thank you." I left her office, this time feeling vindicated.

For the rest of the week, I helped out Dan, just like the early days.

"I've been thinking that maybe I should move on," he said one morning in the coffee room.

"Are you sure? I thought you loved it here."

"I did. I do. Doesn't mean I need to stay."

"But what will you do? I thought you were saving up to move out."

"I am. Oh, I don't know. Maybe I'll just look around for now."

"No harm in looking."

Dan appeared thoughtful, as if weighing up his options. Seemingly content that options at least existed, he perked up and changed the subject.

CHAPTER TWENTY-EIGHT

Brenda wasted no time having a contract drawn up. She delivered it in person to my flat and we spent the morning discussing the business, the clients, and the staff. The notes provided were administrative with likes, dislikes and fetishes committed to memory. She explained in detail how to manage a legitimate escort service and how to deal with any paid activity that took place once the escorting was over.

"How does that sound?" Brenda asked when she'd finished giving me the low-down.

"A little daunting but I think I can do it and I'm really excited."

"You'll be fine." Brenda seemed convinced.

"How does everyone feel about you retiring?" I asked.

"Some are nervous, so I've tried to reassure them that as far as they're concerned, nothing will change. At least for now. This is your business now, Tilly. Your baby. Put your spin on it. People will buy into you. If they can't, then you don't want them."

I thought about that once Brenda had left. This was a business, whether I was selling coffee or company, semolina or sex. It would require marketing, recruitment, and management. A USP. I wouldn't buy a café and keep it the same; I would make it my own, and 'Diamond Escorts' was no different. We were a long way from the 1980s when Brenda started her 'little business'. Undoubtedly, she'd moved with the times but now it was my time. This called for new stationery and maybe an Excel document!

Later that week I met with Michelle, Stella, Jane, and Mo, introducing myself as Brenda's replacement. I practised my speech beforehand and toyed with 'the new Brenda' but that wasn't the case. I wanted them to know that I was different, to make them aware that things might change. Honestly, they seemed okay about it. Maybe they were ready.

The following week I picked up the phone to clients. Professional, discreet calls to inform them that I would be organising the bookings from now on. Yes, they would still have the same lady; no, prices would not be going up; yes, I had all the information I needed.

So far so good.

Introductions made, I felt the scene was set to move forwards. I still wasn't sure 'how' but I'd created numerous mind maps that illustrated the 'what'. I sat on my balcony one evening with a cold glass of wine. The view before me spoke of the possibilities and unknown opportunities ahead. A phone rang. I looked down and picked up the one that Brenda had handed over earlier that day.

"Diamond Escorts. Tilly speaking. How may I help you this evening?"

CHAPTER TWENTY-NINE

A year after taking over the business, I moved into a stunning apartment complex and rented out my old place to Dan. The look on his face when I offered it to him was a treat, and I still get 'balcony selfies' from him. I still have a balcony, but a bigger one now, big enough for one of those rattan sofas.

I use the pool every morning. Three concierges (two Bobs and an Al) offer an amazing round-the-clock service. I seem to be the youngest person in the complex and they've become quite fatherly towards me. I never arrive or leave without one of them asking where I'm off to or telling me to be careful and not to be too late. It's sweet.

I still visit The Grange. In fact, I conduct my own meetings there just like the first one I had with Brenda. I now have five girls working for me and two men. Jane decided it was time to hang up her fluffy handcuffs (her clientele had a penchant for S&M) but the other three chose to hang around. Adding men to the business has proved a popular move. Whether a woman is single or has left her partner at home, sometimes she prefers company on a night out. That might be as a buffer against the company letch or to simply be with someone that makes heads turn.

Although it happened almost by accident, I've really enjoyed adding corporate events to our repertoire. We concentrate on providing a suitable plus one rather than what happens afterwards. We still have our regulars and occasionally I'll get a 'fantasy job', which I love. I stick by Fran's philosophy that 'life is too short' so I'm all about making sure my clients are living their best lives. That could be taking a bit of enviable eye candy to the work's do or being smothered in honey by a stranger because you're not ready to make that particular desire public. We're here for the bizarre, the liberating, the empowering.

Brenda is doing well and although she has taken a complete step back from day-to-day business, she is always there for advice when I need it. Under doctor's orders to live a healthier lifestyle, she has taken up golf. From what my mum has said, I'm not sure Brian is very impressed – not because he doesn't want her there, but because she is already better than him! 'Quite the natural', her coach apparently told her.

She tried to get mum to go along but she wasn't interested. She said she'd rather stay at home and prepare the afternoon tea for when they all get back. If that's what makes mum happy then I'm pleased for her. I just wouldn't want to think the cage door was open, but she'd lost the ability to fly.

Fran is still at LFJ and is loving it. On my recommendation, she asked to work with Sasha and loves the fight for justice in the cutthroat world of death and divorce (Sasha also handles Will disputes).

Fran's dad remarried. At the wedding reception he took me to one side and thanked me for our time together, told me I 'rekindled the spark' and gave him his confidence back. His new wife is lovely. Thankfully, I resisted the urge to tell her how lucky she was; I thought that might be a bit weird coming from somebody my age; probably wouldn't make for good honeymoon pillow talk!

Dan left LFJ to do a fashion degree. He said I'd inspired him to follow his dreams.

Edward and I still see each other once a month. We go out now too and have had a couple of weekends in Europe. I'm not sure where it will take us; I'm on a monthly retainer so the cash exchange is kind of in the background now. One might argue that he's keeping me after all and it might be semantics, but I'd disagree. I have the odd client here and there but I'm more management now. And I've followed Brenda's lead and started investing. This income won't last forever so I'm getting ready for that 'rainy day'. I don't want a health scare to make me realise it's time to slow down.

I've still not felt the need to tell mum and dad exactly what the business entails. I've explained that I provide plus ones for important events for people who don't have the time or the inclination for a relationship and they've not asked for more detail. Sometimes I'll see my dad open his mouth as if to speak but then he'll close it again as if he doesn't know how to frame the question, or maybe he's not sure he wants the answer. Mum just nods and carries on with whatever she happens to be doing. "Sounds like you're having fun," is the most I've got from her and that's fine by me. Maybe she's noticed a shift in my demeanour and doesn't need to know more.

I told my brother and got a few 'nudge-nudge, wink-winks' in return, to which I smiled and responded with a, "Yeah, whatever." He never asks for detail. I don't think he cares that much; his sister is happy, and she always remembers her nephew's birthday.

Life is short and unpredictable. There's a lot out there that we can't control so it's worth taking charge whenever we can. Make that leap of faith, take that job, say yes to that date, leave whatever it is that doesn't fulfil you. Something or someone somewhere will always have your back.

~ THE END OF THE BEGINNING ~